GRAPHIC STORYTELLING

By

Will Eisner

Published

by

POORHOUSE PRESS

Published by
POORHOUSE PRESS
8333 W. McNAB ROAD
TAMARAC, FLORIDA 33321

FIRST PRINTING	**1996**
SECOND PRINTING	**1996**
THIRD PRINTING	**1998**
FOURTH PRINTING	**2000**
FIFTH PRINTING	**2001**

Distributed to the comic book market by:
POORHOUSE PRESS
8333W. Mc Nab Road
Tamarac, FL. 33321
(954) 726-4343

Distributed to the book trade and art/craft
supply markets by:
NORTH LIGHT BOOKS
1507 Dana Avenue
Cincinnati, OH 45207
(800) 289-0963

$22.99 Paperback ISBN #0-9614728-2-0

Library of Congress Catalog Card Number: 95-092606

CONTENTS

ACKNOWLEDGMENTS

This book owes its existence to the students who attended my classes in Sequential Art over 18 years. Their pursuit of excellence and their interest in the standards of the medium helped focus my attention on storytelling and its role in this literary/art form.

To Dave Schreiner, my gratitude for his skillful and patient editing. His years of experience in comic books has been an invaluable aid.

To my wife, Ann, who contributed many hours of logistical support, my appreciation for her interest and endurance during the innumerable changes and type set alterations.

To my son, John, who provided much of the underlying research needed to buttress the postulations common to a book of this kind, my thanks.

To supportive colleagues, Neil Gaiman, Scott McCloud, Tom Inge, and Lucy Caswell, who generously took the time to read the early 'dummy' and provide me with thoughtful opinions and advice, my gratitude.

FOREWORD

In an earlier work, *COMICS AND SEQUENTIAL ART*, I addressed the principles, concept and anatomy of the comics form, as well as the fundamentals of the craft. In this work, I hope to deal with the mission and process of storytelling with graphics.

The effort of artists to tell stories of substance with imagery is not new. In an essay in *BOOKMAN'S WEEKLY* (July 1995) David Beronä reviewed some of the history of this effort. He cited major woodcut artists who, in my opinion, established an historical precedent for modern graphic storytelling. Frans Masereel, a Belgian political cartoonist for *LA FEUILLE,* began producing "novels without words." In 1919 he published *Passionate Journey,* a novel told in 169 woodcuts, last published by Penquin Press, New York, 1988. This book has an introduction by Thomas Mann. The famous author enjoins the reader to accept being "...captivated by the flow of the pictures and...the deeper purer impact than you have ever felt before." Masereel went on to create more than 20 "novels without words." He was followed by Otto Nückel, a German, whose *DESTINY*, a novel in pictures appeared in 1930, published in America by Farrar & Rinehart.

About that time, Lynd Ward also began publishing graphic novels in woodcut form. He dealt with man's spiritual journey through life. In six succeeding books, Ward firmly establishes the architecture of the form. Of greater significance is the resonance of the subjects he undertook. It is these substantial themes that provide encouragement to the aspirations of comics. A sampling of Ward's work is included in this book.

In 1930, Milt Gross, the brilliant American cartoonist, produced a satirical graphic novel, *HE DONE HER WRONG.* It was a spoof of the classic novel done with wordless cartoons. While he didn't have the literary pretensions, or the serious subject intent, of Masereel, Nückel, or Ward, he nevertheless observed the same format. In 1963, it was reprinted in pocket book format by Dell Books. By then, comic books were well established.

Comics are essentially a visual medium composed of images. While words are a vital component, the major dependence for description and narration is on universally understood images, crafted with the intention of imitating or exaggerating reality. The result is often a preoccupation with graphic elements. Page layout, high-impact effects, startling rendering techniques and mind-blowing color can monopolize the creator's attention. The effect of this is that the writer and artist are deflected from the discipline of storytelling construction and become absorbed in a packaging effort. The graphics then *control* the writing and the product descends into little more than literary junk food.

Despite the high visibility and attention that artwork compels, I hold that the story is the most critical component in a comic. Not only is it the intellectual frame on which all artwork rests, but it, more than anything else, helps the work endure. This is a daunting challenge to a medium that has a history of being considered juvenile pap. The task is further compounded by the harsh reality that images and packaging elicit the primary reader response. Nevertheless, comics is a literary/art form, and as it matures, it aspires to recognition as a "legitimate" medium.

The traditional production of comics by a single individual has, over the years, given way to the dominance of teams (writer, artist, inkers, colorists and letterers). While the artist/writer assumes the total storytelling responsibility, the team, on the whole, is involved and must feel connected to the articulation of the story. Writing, as I use it in comics, is not confined to the employment of words. Writing in comics includes all the elements in a seamless mix and becomes part of the mechanics of the art form.

In *STORYTELLING*, the concentration is on a basic understanding of narration with graphics. This book will undertake the examination of storytelling and review the fundamentals of its application in the comics medium.

INTRODUCTION

In our culture, film and comics are the major conveyors of story through imagery. Each employ arranged graphics and text or dialogue. While film and theater have long ago established their credentials, comics still struggle for acceptance, and the art form, after more than ninety years of popular use, is still regarded as a problematic literary vehicle.

The latter half of the 20th century has experienced an alteration in the definition of literacy. The proliferation of the use of images as a communicant was propelled by the growth of a technology that required less in text-reading skills. From road signs to mechanical use instructions, imagery aided words, and at times even supplanted them. Indeed, visual literacy has entered the panoply of skills required for communication in this century. Comics are at the center of this phenomenon.

The rise and establishment of this remarkable reading form in the package we know as comic books occurred over 60 years. From the compilation of pre-published newspaper comic strips, comic book material quickly evolved into complete original stories and then into graphic novels. This last permutation has placed more of a demand for literary sophistication on the artist and writer than ever before.

Since comics are easily read, their reputation for usefulness has been associated with people of low literacy and limited intellectual accomplishment. And, in truth, for decades the story content of comics catered to that audience. Many creators are still content with furnishing little more than titillation and mindless violence. Little wonder that encouragement and acceptance of this medium by the education establishment was for a long time less than enthusiastic.

The predominance of art in the traditional comics format brought more attention to that form than to its literary content. It is hardly surprising, therefore, that comics as a reading form was always assumed to be a threat to literacy, as literacy was defined in the pre-visual /electronic era.

In their influential book *THE MEDIUM IS THE MESSAGE,* Marshall McLuhan and Quenton Fiore point out "... Societies have always been shaped more by the nature of the media by which men communicate than by the content of the communication." This has been the fate of the comics. Its colorful and pictorial format bespoke of simple content.

The years between 1965 and 1990 saw comics beginning to reach for literary content. It started with the confrontational underground movement of artists and writers riding a wave of direct distribution to the market. This was followed by a mushrooming of comic book stores which supplied easy access to a broader spectrum of readers. It was the beginning of the maturation of the medium. At last, comics sought to deal with subject matter that had been regarded as the province of text, live theater or film. Autobiography, social protest, reality-based human relationships and history were some of the subjects now undertaken by comics. The graphic novel that addressed "adult" subjects proliferated. The average age of readers rose. The market for innovation and mature subject matter expanded. Accompanying these changes, a more sophisticated group of creative talents became attracted to the medium and raised its standards.

In this environment, the comic book suffered from the comments of literary critics who found it problematic to determine whether comics could properly deal with serious subjects. This general attitude adversely affected the climate of acceptance.

This epitomizes the challenge facing comic book writers and artists seeking a place in our literary culture. How far comics can go in addressing "serious themes" is an ongoing challenge. Fortunately, the increase in the number of serious artists and writers attracted to comics as a career is testimony to the medium's potential. And it is my conviction that story content will be the propellant of the future of the comic books.

With the beginning of the 1990s, the new literacy became more evident in our western culture, and as Paul Gravett of the *London Daily Telegraph* observed, "There seems to be no limit to the [comics] medium's ambitions....Those accustomed to scanning regular columns of type often have difficulty assimilating the haphazard captions in comics at the same time as jumping from image to image. But to a young generation brought up with television, computers and video games, processing verbal and visual information on several levels at once seems natural, even preferable."

COMICS AS A MEDIUM

Reading in the pure literary sense was mugged on its way to the 21st century by the electronic media, which influenced and changed how we read. Printed text lost its monopoly to another communication technology, film. Aided by electronic transmission, it became the major competitor for readership. With its limited demand on a viewer's cognitive skills, film makes the time-consuming burden of learning to decode and digest words seem obsolete. Film viewers experience countless lifelike incidents of ordained duration as they watch a screen where artificial situations and contrived solutions become integrated into their mental inventory of memories retained from real life experience.

The actors become "real" people. Most important, watching film establishes a rhythm of acquisition. It is a direct challenge to static print. Accustomed to the pace of film, readers grow impatient with long text passages because they have become used to acquiring stories, ideas and information quickly and with little effort. As we know, complex concepts become more easily digested when reduced to imagery. Printed communication as a portable, source of ideas in depth, nevertheless remains a viable and necessary medium. In fact it responds to the challenge of electronic media by merger. A partnership of words with imagery becomes the logical permutation. The resulting configuration is called comics and it fills a gap between print and film.

In his fine book *UNDERSTANDING COMICS*, Scott McCloud aptly described comics as "a vessel which can hold any number of ideas and images." In a wider view we must consider this vessel as a communicator. It is in every sense a singular form of reading

The reading process in comics is an extension of text. In text alone the process of reading involves word-to-image conversion. Comics accelerates that by providing the image. When properly executed, it goes beyond conversion and speed and becomes a seamless whole. In every sense, this misnamed form of reading is entitled to be regarded as literature because the images are employed as a language. There is a recognizable relationship to the iconography and pictographs of oriental writing

When this language is employed as a conveyance of ideas and information, it separates itself from mindless visual entertainment. This makes comics a storytelling medium.

NOTE: Certain terms are used throughout. They are:

GRAPHIC NARRATIVE
A generic description of any narration that employs image to transmit an idea. Film and comics both engage in graphic narrative.

COMICS
The printed arrangement of art and balloons in sequence, particularly as in comic books.

STORYTELLER
The writer or person in control of the narration.

SEQUENTIAL ART
A train of images deployed in sequence.

1

THE STORY OF STORYTELLING

The telling of a story lies deep in the social behavior of human groups -- ancient and modern. Stories are used to teach behavior within the community, to discuss morals and values, or to satisfy curiosity. They dramatize social relations and the problems of living, convey ideas or act out fantasies. The telling of a story requires skill.

In primitive times, the teller of stories in a clan or tribe served as entertainer, teacher and historian. Storytelling preserved knowledge by passing it from generation to generation. This mission has continued into modern times. The storyteller must first have something to tell, and then must be able to master the tools to relay it.

The earliest storytellers probably used crude images buttressed with gestures and vocal sounds which later evolved into language. Over the centuries, technology provided paper, printing machines and electronic storage and transmission devices. As these developments evolved, they affected the narrative arts.

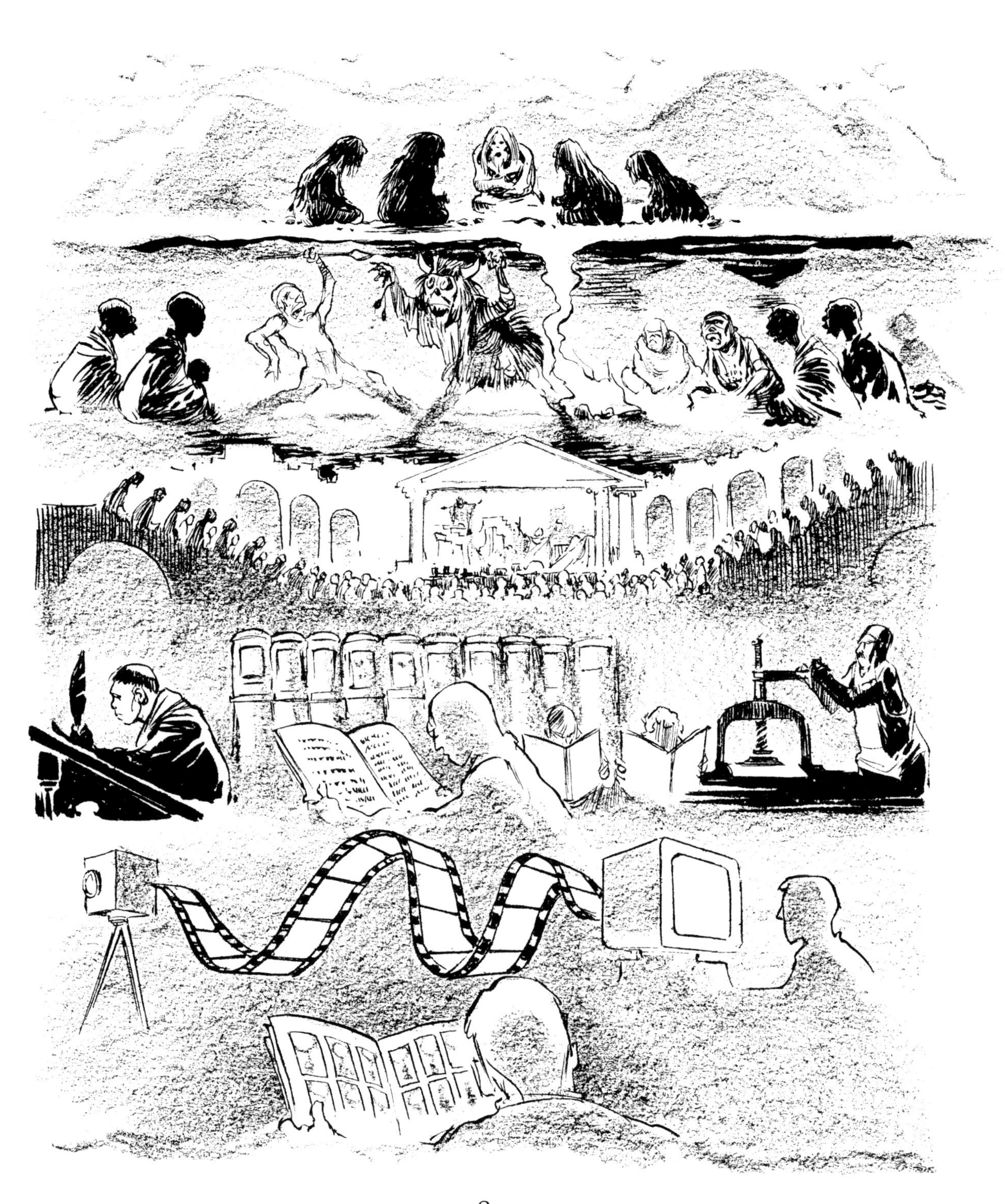

2

WHAT IS A STORY?

All stories have a structure. A story has a beginning, an end, and a thread of events laid upon a framework that holds it together. Whether the medium is text, film or comics, the skeleton is the same. The style and manner of its telling may be influenced by the medium but the story itself abides.

The structure of a story can be diagrammed with many variations, because it is subject to different patterns between its beginning and end. A structure is useful as a guide to maintaining control of the telling.

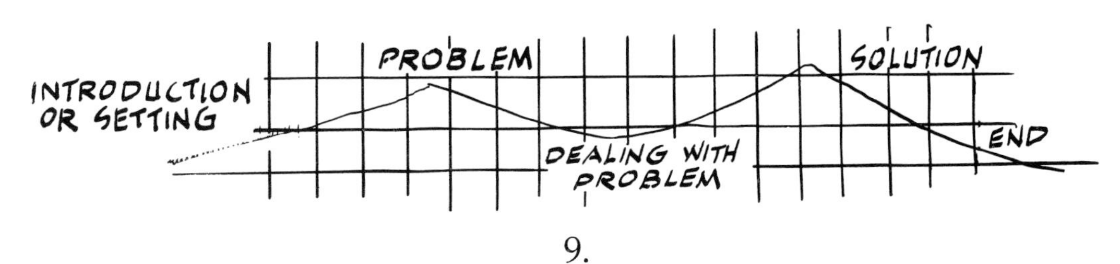

This is a story in the abstract. At this point, it is still a lot of thoughts, memories, fantasies, and ideas, floating around in one's head, waiting for a structure.

It becomes a story when told in an arranged and purposeful order. The basic principles of narration are the same whether told orally or visually.

THE FUNCTION OF A STORY

The story form is a vehicle for conveying information in an easily absorbed manner. It can relate very abstract ideas, science, or unfamiliar concepts by the analogous use of familiar forms or phenomena.

BUT I CAN ALSO TELL YOU STORIES TO MAKE YOU LAUGH!
YEAH, YEAH, I COULD USE A LITTLE ENTERTAINMENT
SURE, LIFE AROUND HERE IS PRETTY GRIM Y'KNOW
I COULD ALSO TELL YOU A SCARY STORY!
GEE!
I DON'T KNOW WHY... BUT I KINDA LIKE BEING SCARED... C'MON TELL US ONE!
NOW I MUST FIGURE OUT HOW TO TELL IT!!

3

TELLING A STORY

There are different ways of telling a story. Technology provides many vehicles of transmission, but fundamentally there are only two major ways: words (oral or written) or images. Sometimes the two are combined.

STORIES TOLD WITH PRINT

Through the first half of the 20th century, print dominated as a vehicle of communication. While film and electronics have challenged its superiority, print will nevertheless maintain its importance. Stories told with graphic narration must deal with transmission. This has an influence on the manner in which the story is told and will influence the story itself. It is at this point that the storyteller comes in contact with the marketplace.

Readers and viewers identify content with its package. Comics readers expect printed comics to come in a familiar package. A story told in an unconventional format may be perceived differently. The format has an important influence in graphic storytelling.

STORIES TOLD WITH IMAGERY

For the purpose of this discussion, an "image" is the memory of an object or experience recorded by a narrator either mechanically (photograph) or by hand (drawing). In comics, images are generally impressionistic. Usually, they are rendered with economy in order to facilitate their usefulness as a language. Because experience precedes analysis, the intellectual digestive process is accelerated by the imagery provided by comics.

Imagery used as a language has some drawbacks. It is the element of comics that has always provoked resistance to its acceptance as serious reading. Critics also sometimes accuse it of inhibiting imagination.

Static images have limitations. They do not articulate abstractions or complex thought easily.

But images define in absolute terms. They are specific.

Images in print or film transmit with the speed of sight.

4

IMAGES AS NARRATIVE TOOLS

STEREOTYPICAL IMAGES

In the dictionary, *stereotype* is defined as an idea or character that is standardized in a conventional form, without individuality. As an adjective, *stereotypical* applies to that which is hackneyed. Stereotype has a bad reputation not only because it implies banality but because of its use as a weapon of propaganda or racism. Where it simplifies and categorizes an inaccurate generalization, it may be harmful, or at the least offensive. The actual word comes from the method used to mold duplicate plates in letterpress printing. These definitions notwithstanding, the stereotype is a fact of life in the comics medium. It is an accursed necessity -- a tool of communication that is an inescapable ingredient in most cartoons. Given the narrative function of the medium, this should not be surprising.

Comic book art deals with recognizable reproductions of human conduct. Its drawings are a mirror reflection, and depend on the reader's stored memory of experience to visualize an idea or process quickly. This makes necessary the simplification of images into repeatable symbols. Ergo, stereotypes.

In comics, stereotypes are drawn from commonly accepted physical characteristics associated with an occupation. These become icons and are used as part of the language in graphic storytelling.

In film, there is plenty of time to develop a character within an occupation. In comics, there is little time or space. The image or caricature must settle the matter instantly.

For example, in creating a doctor prototype, it is useful to adopt a compound of characteristics that the reader will accept. Usually this image is drawn from both social experience and what the reader thinks a doctor ought to look like.

Where the plot is arranged to support it, the standardized "doctor look" can be abandoned in favor of a type suitable to the story environment.

The art of creating a stereotypical image for the purpose of storytelling requires a familiarity with the audience and a recognition that each society has its own ingrown set of accepted stereotypes. But there are those that transcend cultural boundaries.

The comics' creator can now count on a global distribution of his work. To communicate well, the storyteller must be conversant with what is universally valid.

STANDARDS OF REFERENCE

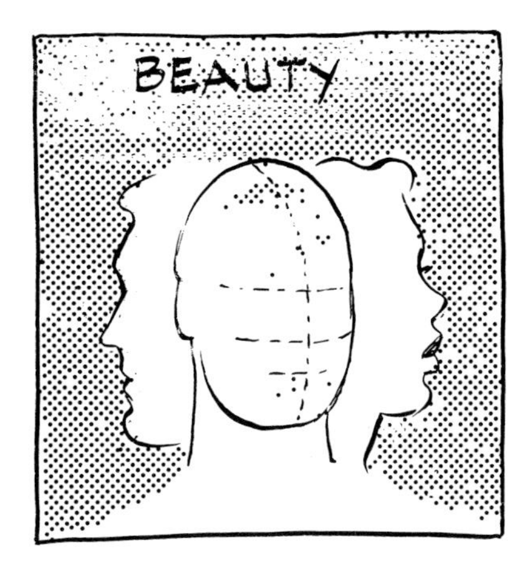

ROMANCE

Certain human characteristics are recognizable by physical appearance. In each of the above, the reader evokes a message out of the stereotypical image. In this example, the stereotype of a strong man reinforces romantic believability while an incongruity that provokes humor is conveyed by using a stereotype of a nerd.

In devising actors, it is important to understand why the use of commonly accepted types can evoke a viewer's reflexive response. I believe that modern humans still retain instincts developed as primordials. Possibly the recognition of a dangerous person or responses to threatening postures are residuals of a primitive existence. Perhaps in the early experience with animal life, people learned which facial configurations and postures were either threatening or friendly. It was important for survival to recognize instantly which animal was dangerous.

There is evidence of this in the successful readability of animal-based images which comics commonly employs when seeking to evoke character recognition.

In graphic storytelling, there is little time or space for character development. The use of these animal-based stereotypes speeds the reader into the plot and gives the teller reader-acceptance for the action of his characters.

SYMBOLISM

Just as stereotype employs images of people who can be easily identified in comics or film, objects have their own vocabulary in the visual language of comics.

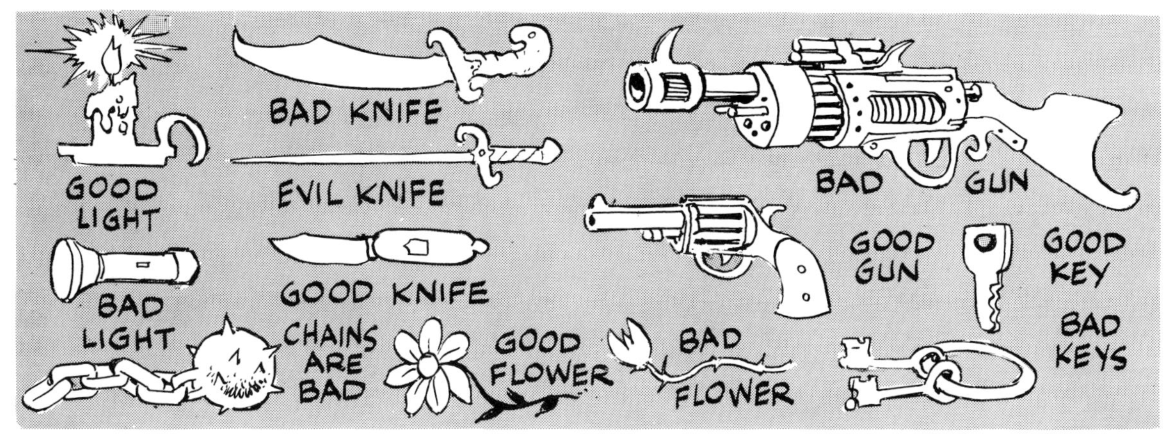

There are some objects which have instant significance in graphic storytelling. When they are employed as modifying adjectives or adverbs, they provide the storyteller with an economical narrative device.

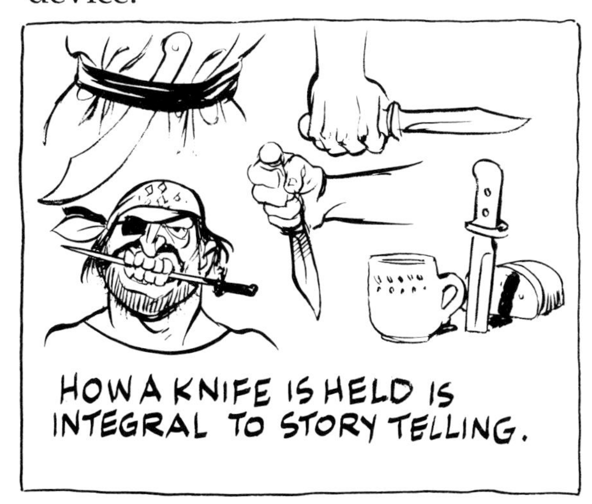

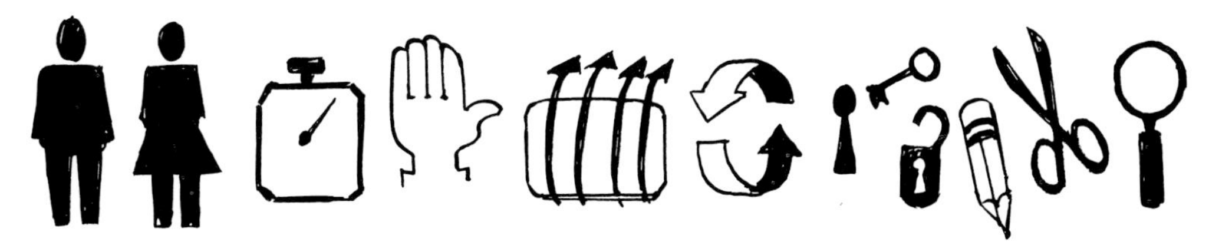

Computers often use symbols to instruct their operators. These are derived from objects familiar to people in a technical society.

Apparel is symbolic. It can tell instantly the strength, character, occupation and intent of its wearer. How it is worn may also convey a signal to the reader.

In comics, as in film, symbolic objects not only narrate but heighten the emotional reaction of the reader.

In this story, the selection of a doll and broken signs evoke sympathy because they are commonly identified with non-combatants. Left lying in the snow broken and abandoned, they not only testify to the innocence of the victims, but solicit the reader's condemnation of the killers.

5

ALL KINDS OF STORIES

A wide range of stories can be told in the graphic medium but the method of telling a story must be specific to its message.

TELLING STORIES TO INSTRUCT

A process is most easily taught when it is wrapped in an interesting "package"... a story, for example. As comics demonstrated the capacity to marshal technical elements in a disciplined order, they found ready patronage.

This demonstrates the order of thinking when an instructional comic is created.

TELLING A HOW-TO STORY

Stories that seek to teach something are usually structured to center on the process. Skills are learned by imitation.

TELLING THE PLOTLESS STORY

When high-tech layout and visual pyrotechnics dominate a comic, the result is often a very simple plot.

To a reader interested in the excitement of graphic effects or bravura art, this is quite enough. In fact, a plot with too much 'density' can be an impediment. In order to successfully satisfy this, the artist requires from the writer little more than a plot that centers on a single problem, as in plots that center on pursuit or acts of vengeance. Most often, the solution is so uncomplicated, violent action and *special effect* art must sustain interest. The art becomes the story, as in tapestries.

TELLING THE ILLUSTRATED STORY

During the mid-'70s, propelled and enabled by great advances in printing and reproduction technology, the illustrated story attracted the interest of comic book artists, writers and publishers. This format was not new, but its renaissance offered highly-skilled illustrators and sophisticated writers a compatible vehicle.

In this form of graphic storytelling, the writer and artist retain their sovereignty because the story comes from the text and is embellished by the art. The leisurely rhythm of this kind of graphic storytelling allows the reader time to dwell on the art alone, which is mainly concerned with itself. The artist can freely use oil, watercolor, wood engravings or manipulated photography. The skill demands of these techniques are often so great that the art might overwhelm the story.
In the market place, however, it makes for a very attractive package and conforms to the traditional "book" concept.

Little did she know then that she would rue it...
And when she killed him the escape to Europe did not free her of his hold on her.
For the Baron grew more monstrous as each year passed.

So Amy returned, drawn to it by some strong, magnetic force.

The castle stood alone, steeped in a shroud of evil spawned centuries ago. Amy's new life at Margate was uneventful until one day a cold wind seeped into her chamber.

She knew...

The time had come.

...out of the dank darkness of the castle's corridors stepped the nobleman of the night ...

The cry was muffled and the deed done with the swift certainty of a curse fulfilled!

Margate Castle remains the dark dominion of its undead 'Black Baron'.

THE SYMBOLISTIC STORY

In this story, the fulcrum of the plot is two symbols, a daisy and a spiked ball. These symbols serve to establish the premise within a symbolistic plot and symbolic characters.

COUGH COUGH
VOTING BOOTH
I WANT TO REGISTER TO VOTE
WHAT
WHAT A WASTE OF TIME... YOU'RE THE ONLY MAN IN THE COUNTRY WHO WILL VOTE TOMORROW YOU FOOL, YOU FOOL ZEBLON
THAT NIGHT
AND SO... AS THE LAST VOTE TAKES PLACE TOMORROW THE COUNTRY WILL GO FORWARD WITH ITS NEW FLAG INTO AN ERA OF ORDER AND DICIPLINE... GOOD NIGHT!
COUGH COUGH
KNOCK KNOCK
COME IN?
COUGH
ZEBLON YOU CANT VOTE TOMORROW!! IT WILL EMBARRASS US!!
WE'RE YOUR RELATIVES, YOU MUST CONSIDER US!
TELL ME DO YOU WANT THE KIND OF FLAG THEY PROPOSE??
WELL, NO...
NOT REALLY
THEN HOW WILL THEY KNOW UNLESS YOU SAY SO...
BUT IF WE SAY SO... THEN WE CREATE DISSENT
AND THAT'S NOT VERY ORDERLY
BUT I DONT LIKE THE NEW FLAG..

QUIET, ALBERT! SHHHH!
BUT OUR NATIONAL FLOWER IS IMPORTANT TO US...
HE'S RIGHT, WHY SHOULDN'T IT BE ON OUR FLAG...
AN IRON BALL IS NOT A FIT SYMBOL FOR US...
BUT THE GOVERNMENT WANTS IT...
WHO IS THE GOVERNMENT ???
ACTUALLY WE ARE THE GOVERNMENT ALBERT!!
PRESIDENTS AND PRIME MINISTERS ARE ONLY HIRED BY US TO RUN THE MACHINERY OF GOVERNMENT...
SO, WE SHOULD TELL THEM WHAT WE WANT RIGHT.
AND... THAT'S WHAT-VOTING-IS ... ITS A RIGHT NOT A PRIVILEGE... COUGH
ZEBLON, ZEBLON... WHAT'S THE MATTER?
GET OUT ALL OF YOU.. LET ME BE.
HE'LL NEVER MAKE IT
POOR OL' ZEBLON ITS HIS WEAK HEART AGAIN
HE SHOULDN'T BE POLITICAL IN HIS CONDITION..
THE WHOLE THING IS A WASTE OF TIME
4

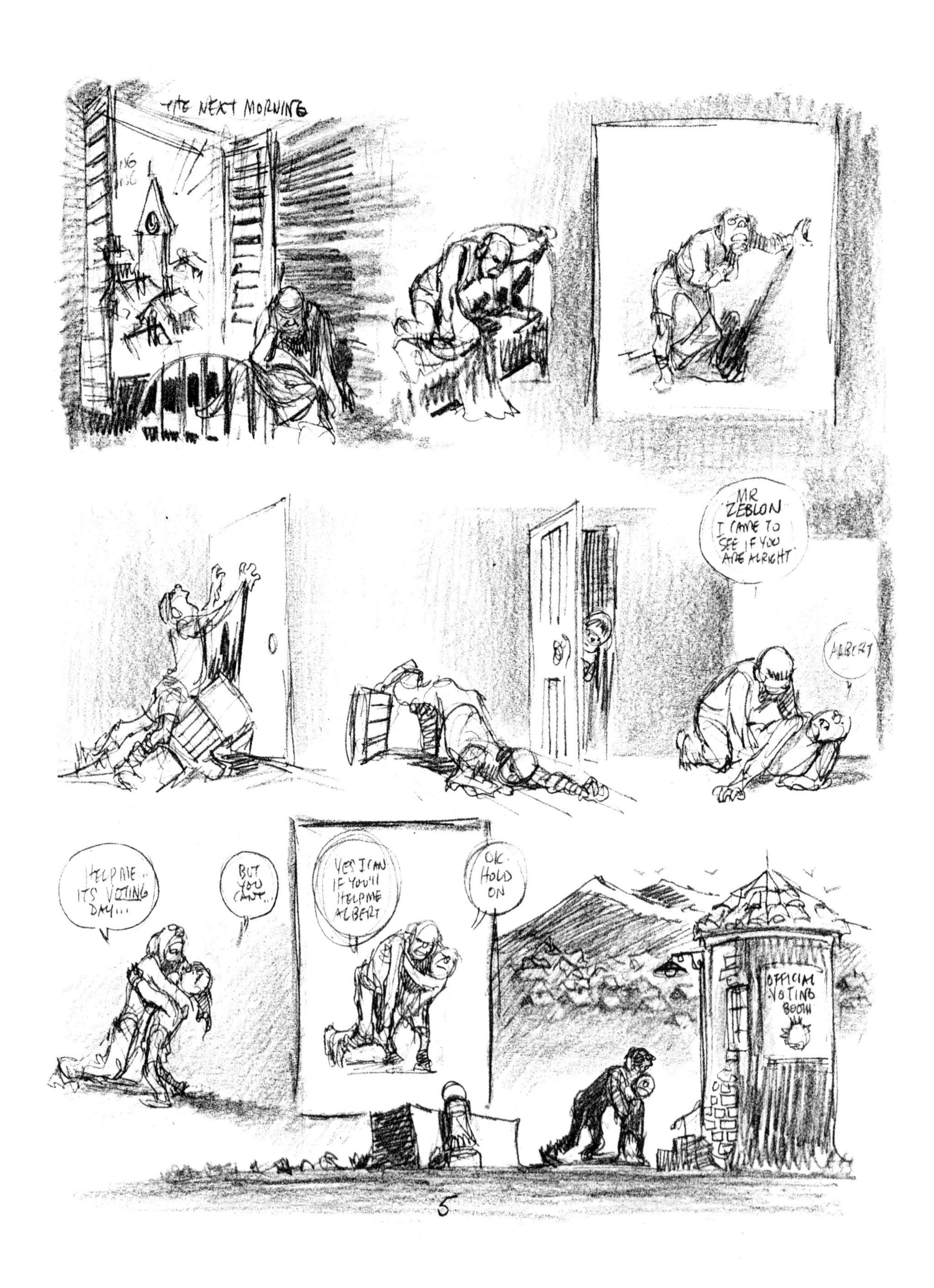
THE NEXT MORNING
MR ZEBLON I CAME TO SEE IF YOU ARE ALRIGHT
ALBERT
HELP ME... ITS VOTING DAY...
BUT YOU CAN'T...
YES I CAN IF YOU'll HELP ME ALBERT
OK. HOLD ON
OFFICIAL VOTING BOOTH
5

WHAT'S HAPPENED WHERE'S EVERYONE GOING?
TO THE VOTING BOOTH
ZEBLON IS VOTING
ALBERT DID ZEBLON VOTE
ZEBLON COME OUT!
ZEBLON NAUGHT COME OUT AND TELL US HOW YOU VOTED
H.HE... CANT
HE VOTED... AND THEN HE... DIED..
HA HA HA HA HA
RIDICULOUS!! AN OLD MAN VOTES AND DIES ON THE SPOT... AND YOU THINK ITS SERIOUS?? HA HA
YES, ITS ONLY ONE VOTE AFTER ALL
MARTYRS, ARE A SERIOUS MATTER GENERAL
THE EFFECT ON THE PUBLIC IS CERTAINLY SERIOUS

YOU DON'T SEEM TO UNDERSTAND... HIS ACT RAISED THE ISSUE OF VOTING TO A NEW IMPORTANCE -
THE PUBLIC IS AROUSED
DAMN THE PUBLIC.... WE'RE IN CONTROL
'PERHAPS' BUT NOW THE SEEDS OF AN OPPOSITION HAS BEEN PLANTED!
THIS OPENS UP THE OPPORTUNITY FOR ANOTHER FACTION -
ANOTHER FACTION?
YES AND SOMEBODY WILL TAKE ADVANTAGE OF THIS AND LEAD THE OPPOSITION!
REALLY?
WHO?
US!
!

THIS MEANS A BLOODY FIGHT... THAT COULD LEAVE THE COUNTRY IN RUINS!
AN AWFUL IDEA
THERE IS A SOLUTION.'
RESTORE ELECTIONS
WHAT IF I LOSE!
UNDER A FREE ELECTION SYSTEM. LOSERS HAVE A CHANCE TO WIN IN THE NEXT ELECTION!
AND SO.... THE LITTLE COUNTRY RESTORED ELECTIONS AND THE RIGHT TO VOTE WAS RETURNED TO THE PEOPLE... NOW, THEY HAD TO PARTICIPATE IN GOVERNING THEM SELVES... WHICH OF COURSE BROUGHT DISSENT - AND ALL THE OTHER UNCOMFORTABLE THINGS CONNECTED WITH EXERCISING THIS BASIC, AND IRREVOCABLE HUMAN RIGHT -
UNTIDY SYSTEM
MAYBE BUT ITS BETTER THAN ANYTHING YET DEVISED!

TELLING THE SLICE- OF- LIFE STORY

A slice-of-life story generally extracts an interesting segment from human experience and examines it.

The storyteller selects an event of interest which can stand alone. The writer counts on the life experience or the imagination of the reader to supply the impact of the story. The reader's appreciation hinges on the telling of it. It requires that the artist portrays believable acting. Since characters are dealing with internal emotions, subtle postures and gestures must be true-to-life, instantly recognizable. Powerhouse layouts or excessive rendering technique, which can overwhelm and distract the reader and dominate the story, are counter-productive in this form.

Below are the critical elements of a story that are never made explicit to the reader. In the story that follows, they are implied and are an invisible part of the narrative.

WHAT HAPPENED BEFORE

PRITZIK STARTED OUT (WITH HIS WIFE'S MONEY) PEDDLING DRESSES... SOON HE MADE ENOUGH MONEY TO START UP!

HE OPENED HIS OWN COMPANY BUT WITH LIMITED CAPITAL HE COULD ONLY HIRE LOW GRADE WORKERS

SO IT WAS A NEVER ENDING STRUGGLE TO SURVIVE... IT MADE PRITZIK A BITTER MAN WITH A WEAK, MARGINAL, BUSINESS.

WHAT HAPPENED AFTER

THE NEWS OF HIS SUCCESS BROUGHT A MERGER OFFER.

BUT THE CONTROLLING STOCK WAS IN THE HANDS OF GIPPLE...

WHO WINDS UP IN CONTROL OF THE COMPANY

A SMALL BUSINESS
BY Will Eisner
"A small business is a big business that ain't yet big."
A. PITZIK
SINCE THE BEGINNING, 14 YEARS ALREADY, GIPPLE THE GIMP DELIVERED SAMPLES FOR THE STYLESH DRESS MFG. Co. (A. Pitzik, prop.) THROUGH RAIN, HEAT AND SNOW FAITHFULLY! SO WHAT ELSE IS THERE TO SAY-WHAT ELSE IS AN UNSKILLED SHLEP GOOD FOR... EH??
STYLESH DRESS

I DELIVERED TO ACME BOSS... IT'S RAINING OUT!
SO DON'T STAND THERE!! RIGHT AWAY TAKE THE STOUTS OVER TO MERRYWETHER... THEM SAMPLES GOTTA BE IN THEIR SHOWROOM BEFORE THE BUYERS COME.
CLACK CLACK CLACK CLACK CLACK
I'M LIVING ON THE BRINK OF BANKRUPTCY- AND HE'S KREKTSING ABOUT RAIN!
CLACK CLACK CLACK CLACK
A RUNNER-WHAT DOES HE KNOW ABOUT BUSINESS? -THE AGGRAVATION..!!
SLAM
BZZZZ
CLACK CLACK
PITZIK IN?? TELL HIM IT'S ROCCO.
MR. ROCCO TO SEE YOU!!
GO RIGHT IN!
CLACK CLACK CLACK CLACK
...BEFORE YOU SAY ONE WORD, ROCCO-LEMME TELL YOU... I CAN'T MEET THE PAYMENT... I'M ALL TIED UP IN INVENTORY!!
CLICK

THE SEASON'S JUST BEGINNING, GIMME TIME!
SIGH YA TOLEME LAST MONTH, 'N THE MONTH BEFORE... SIGH
PITZIK, PITZIK... I GOT OBLIGATIONS, TOO. ...MY PEOPLE, THEY DON'T WAIT—IF I DON'T COLLECT, BAD THINGS HAPPEN!
BAD THINGS, PITZIK!!
CRAK
I GOTTA GIVE THEM SOMETHING.
OKAY, OKAY...
LOOK, ROCCO... I'LL GIVE YOU THE COMPANY'S STOCK. SEE... I'LL SIGN IT OVER—THEN YA CAN FILL IN ANYBODY'S NAME AND THEY'LL OWN THE WHOLE BUSINESS!
...YOU'LL GIVE IT BACK TO ME WHEN I PAY OFF THE LOAN!
MAYBE...
MAYBE? MAYBE?? WHY YOU NO GOOD BUM! YOU GOT 14 YEARS OF MY LIFE IN YOUR HANDS!
?!
?

OUTTA MY WAY, JERK ☼ GAGH!
BANG

I DELIVERED T' MERRYWETHER, BOSS... CAN I GO HOME NOW? I'M WET FROM THE RAIN!
AGAIN WITH THE RAIN... GIPPLE, CANTCHA SEE I'M HURT!

SHLEMIEL... I GOTTA RAISE MONEY TO GET BACK MY **STOCK**. ...**ANYBODY** SIGNS THEIR **NAME** ON THAT STOCK **OWNS** THIS COMPANY... AAAH! WHY AM I TELLING YOU?

YOU STAY!! — AND **LOCK** UP! I GOTTA GO...
YES, BOSS!

Gipple

TELLING A LIFE STORY

This story employs a single event in a single day to define a man and his life. The storyteller is always confronted with the difficulty of selecting a revealing incident that will withstand the reader's judgment of what is believable.

THE WINNER

SINCE DAWN, SPECTATORS HAVE BEEN STATIONING THEMSELVES ALONG THE ROUTE, HOPING FOR A GLIMPSE OF THE RUNNERS AS THEY GO BY. SUPPORTERS ARE GENERALLY SMALL GROUPS OR INDIVIDUALS HOPING TO SINGLE OUT A FRIEND IN THE HORDE OF STARTERS. THEY ARE AS UNREMARKABLE AS THE CONTESTANTS THEMSELVES, WHOSE PRIVATE REASONS FOR COMPETING IN THIS UNOFFICIAL MEET WITH ITS VAGUE REWARD REMAIN THE UNTOLD STORY OF THIS EVENT.

AS THE RUNNERS ASSEMBLE, WE CAN SEE A FEW FAMILIAR FACES HERE AND THERE AMONG THE CLERKS, SHOPKEEPERS, LAWYERS, BROKERS AND OTHERS.... AHH,... THERE IS....

BENNY!
BENNY... YOU'RE CRAZY! YOU CAN'T DO THIS!
!
OH, HI, CLARA, SO, YOU CAME AFTER ALL ?!
BENNY, YOU NEVER, EVER RAN, OR JOGGED - EVEN FOR A BUS... IT'S 28 MILES... 28 MILES!
I KNOW THAT...
I ALREADY SIGNED UP... SO, THAT'S IT!
HERE, CLARA, WOULD YOU TIE MY GLASSES ON IN BACK!?
BUT WHY, BENNY, WHY? WHY?
...WILL YOU TAKE CARE OF MY THINGS ?
SURE, BENNY.

THEY'RE OFF, FOLKS!! 5000 RUNNERS
A HUMAN TIDAL WAVE SURGING DOWN THE AVENUE
A MASS OF DETERMINATION!

BENNY! THEY'RE ALL PASSING YOU! COME ON!
I'LL SEE YOU UPTOWN, BENNY!
...IT'S A SHAME YOU QUIT HIGH SCHOOL, BENNY, YOU HAVE ONLY ONE MORE YEAR TO GO...
... YOU MEAN...YOU'RE NOT GOING TO TRY FOR THAT PROMOTION??!!... BENNY, BENNY, YOU'LL BE STUCK IN THAT SHIPPING DEPARTMENT FOREVER...

WELL, FOLKS,...THE 15TH CITY MARATHON HAS BECOME **HISTORY**...
THIS YEAR, THE WINNER IS TOR HUGEN WHO CAME ALL THE WAY FROM EUROPE TO FINISH WELL AHEAD OF THE FIELD...
....AS NIGHT FALLS, A QUIET SETTLES ON THE EMPTIED STREETS...
IT'S ALL OVER, FOLKS... GOOD NIGHT!

BENNY... IT'S TWO O'CLOCK IN THE MORNING!!
BENNY, BENNY... IT'S ALL OVER!
LEGGO!
WHERE'S THE LINE
THERE... BENNY, NEXT BLOCK.
YOU DID IT, BENNY, YOU DID IT!!
CLARA... I GOT... SOMETHING TO ASK YOU.
YES, BENNY, WHAT?
WILL YOU MARRY ME?

6

THE READER

To whom are you telling your story?

The answer to this question precedes the telling because it is a fundamental concern of delivery. The reader's profile — his experience and cultural characteristics — must be reckoned with before the teller can successfully narrate the tale. Successful communication depends on the teller's own memory of experience and visual vocabulary.

EMPATHY

Perhaps the most basic of human characteristics is empathy. This trait can be used as a major conduit in the delivery of a story. Its exploitation can be counted upon as one of the teller's tools.

Empathy is a visceral reaction of one human being to the plight of another. The ability to "feel" the pain, fear or joy of someone else enables the storyteller to evoke an emotional contact with the reader. We see ample evidence of this in movie theaters where people weep over the grief of an actor, who is pretending while in an event that is not really happening.

The wincing with vicarious pain when observing someone being hit is, according to some scientists, evidence of fraternal behavior, the work of a neural psychological mechanism developed in humanoids from very early on. On the other hand, researchers argue that empathy results from our ability to run through our minds a narrative of the sequence of a particular event. This not only suggests a cognitive capacity but an innate ability to understand a story.

There is a whole body of clinical studies to support the conclusion that humans learn from infancy to watch and learn to interpret gestures, postures, imagery and other non-verbal social signals. From these, they can deduce meanings and motives like love, pain, and anger, among others.

The relevance of all this to graphic storytelling becomes even more apparent with the claims by scientists that the evolution of hominids' ability to read the intentions of others in their group involves their visual-neural equipment. This was possible , they contend, because as the visual system evolved it became more connected to the emotional centers of the brain. It helps, therefore, for an image maker to understand that all human muscles, in one way or another are controlled by the brain.

Based on the understanding of empathy's cause and effect, we can then come to the fashioning of a reader-teller contract.

THE "CONTRACT"

At the outset of the telling of a story, whether oral, written, or graphic, there is an understanding between the teller and the listener, or reader. The teller expects that the audience will comprehend, while the audience expects the author will deliver something that is comprehensible. In this agreement, the burden is on the teller. This is a basic rule of communication.

In comics the reader is expected to understand things like implied time, space, motion, sound and emotions. In order to do this, a reader must not only draw on visceral reactions but make use of an accumulation of experience as well as reasoning.

CONTROL OF READER

A major element in the reader-teller contract is the struggle to maintain reader interest. The devices used in the telling bind the reader to the storytelling.

For the storyteller this is a matter of control. Once the reader's attention is seized it cannot be allowed to escape.

The key to reader-control is relevance to his interest and understanding. There are a few fundamental themes (of which there are hundreds of permutations) which can be called universal. These include stories that satisfy curiosity about little known areas of life; stories that provide a view of human behavior under various conditions; stories that depict fantasies; stories that surprise; and stories that amuse.

In comics, reader control is attained in two stages — attention and retention. Attention is accomplished by provocative and attractive imagery. Retention is achieved by the logical and intelligible arrangement of the images.

SURPRISE, SHOCK AND READER RETENTION

Surprise is an often used element in all storytelling. In the graphic language, the use of surprise requires stagecraft. In film it is achieved by a sudden and unexpected happening or appearance, usually unforeseen. This is reasonably easy to do because the audience is a spectator that can see only the events shown exactly in the order in which they are displayed. For example, sudden appearance is a commonly used device to achieve surprise or shock.

In comics, because the reader is in control of the acquisition, it is more difficult to surprise, shock or retain his interest. Sometimes a comic teller may try to use the turning of a page to achieve a surprise. But unless the reader is disciplined (does not skip ahead), he can elude the teller's grasp and "see what happens next." Aside from unexpected turns in the thread of a story, surprising the reader on a visual level remains a major problem.

In comics, the solution is to *surprise the character* with whom the reader is involved.

An example of an attempt to surprise the reader is demonstrated in the following sequence. The reader is led to expect a normal exchange between two unimpaired people over several pages. Of course, there is still the possibility that by "flipping" ahead, the surprise will be mitigated. So no attempt is made to surprise the reader with a "shock" graphic. It is left to the characters to act it out.

In this case, we have two surprises. One, we present a seemingly active, even athletic, man and reveal only later his infirmity (speechlessness). Two, we reveal the girl as crippled only after allowing her to react to his speechlessness in the manner of a "normal" person.

While the contrivance is choreographed, the reader is involved by the reaction of the characters. Without those reactions, the surprise would fail.

CALL THE POLICE!
WELCOME TO MY GARDEN!

OH DON'T BE AFRAID... I'M QUITE ALONE HERE... MY GRANDMOTHER INSIDE IS AN INVALID!
OH, YOU'RE SAFE HERE, FOR YOU'VE FALLEN INTO A MAGIC GARDEN!
HEY! ANYBODY SEEN A GUY COME DOWN THE FIRE ESCAPE?!
QUICKLY HIDE UNDER THAT BUSH UNTIL THEY STOP LOOKING!
NO!!
YOU CAN COME OUT NOW.... OH PRINCE OF THE POOR!

I KNEW YOU WOULD COME FOR ME... AND HERE YOU ARE: A PRINCE FROM AN ENCHANTED KINGDOM OF THE POOR!
OH, OH, DON'T BE SURPRISED MY ROSES TOLD ME. I TRUST THEM!
EVERYTHING HERE IN THIS GARDEN IS MAGICAL.... WONDERFUL THINGS REALLY DO HAPPEN!
ACTUALLY I AM AN ENCHANTED PRINCESS... YOU HAVE COME TO CARRY ME OFF!
YOU WILL TAKE ME TO YOUR KINGDOM! THERE WE WILL MARRY AND LIVE HAPPILY EVER AFTER!
AH... BUT YOU'VE LET ME BABBLE LONG ENOUGH... MY NAME IS ROWENA WHAT IS YOURS??
GLAK

AHHA!! I UNDERSTAND! ... YOU CAN'T TALK!
... I SEE... A CRUEL KING CAUSED A WICKED WITCH TO LAY A CURSE ON YOU!
.. BUT IT WILL TURN OUT HAPPILY ..... YOU WILL LIVE HERE WITH ME... .. WE WILL MARRY ONE DAY!
AND IN TIME WE WILL BREAK THE SPELL AND YOU WILL SPEAK AGAIN!
WAIT WAIT
DON'T GO... PLEASE!
IF YOU TRY TO LEAVE THE GARDEN I SHALL SCREAM... AND THE POLICE WILL COME AND....

DIALOGUE
THE READER AS ACTOR

The comics medium does not have sound, music, or motion so this requires readers to participate in the acting out of the story. The dialogue, therefore, becomes a critical element. Where dialogue is not furnished, it requires that the storyteller depend on the reader's life experience to supply the speech that amplifies the intercourse between the actors.

In depicting a silent sequence of interaction, the comic teller must be sure to employ gestures and postures easily identifiable with the dialogue being played out in a reader's mind.

READER VS. DIALOGUE

In this sequence, the reader is forced to participate by supplying unspoken dialogue. In this case, the last panel supplies all the words needed. Used often in films, this device has the effect of compressing a sequence which might otherwise lose rhythm and credulity. In cases like this, the reader with some life experience can supply the dialogue.

DIALOGUE VS. IMAGE

In reality, action precedes words. In comics, therefore, the dialogue is actually conceived after the action is devised.

In comics, no one really knows for certain whether the words are read before or after viewing the picture. We have no real evidence that they are read simultaneously. There is a different cognitive process between reading words and pictures. But in any event, the image and the dialogue give meaning to each other -- a vital element in graphic storytelling.

DIALOGUE VS. ACTION

Because a flow of action immediately takes on a rhythm, the dialogue must accommodate the pageantry. Balloons can impede flow by making unreasonable demands on the reader's sense of reality -- and the storyteller's credibility.

There is a demand on the reader to maintain a sense of time. When there is an exchange of dialogue, time passes. Here is an "exchange" timed in seconds.

There is an almost geometric relationship between the duration of dialogue and the endurance of the posture from which it emanates. In this exchange, there is a perceived time lapse between the dialogue and the action. An actor gets into position and speaks his line. The other actor assumes a posture before responding. All this takes place in a matter of seconds.

Here is what happens when the comic teller allows an exchange of dialogue to emanate from the same image. There is a saving of space but it is at the expense of credibility.

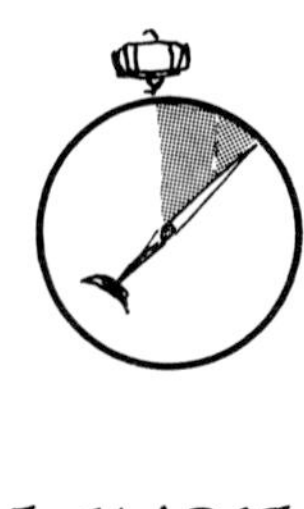

TIME ELAPSE BASED ON THE ENDURANCE OF THE DIALOGUE EXCHANGE

A MORE ECONOMICAL SOLUTION THAT PRESERVES THE BOND BETWEEN DIALOGUE AND ACTION.

If there is an applicable formula, it would be to ordain that the dialogue terminates the endurance of the image. The logic of this is that a protracted exchange of dialogue cannot be realistically supported by unmoving static images.

DIALOGUE AND THE READER

Given the absence of sound, the dialogue in balloons acts as a script to guide the reader in reciting it mentally. The style of lettering and the emulation of accents are the clues enabling the reader to read it with the emotional nuances the comic teller intended. This is essential to the credibility of the imagery. There are commonly accepted lettering characteristics which imply sound level and emotion.

STORY MOMENTUM

When the reader becomes involved with a story and is familiar with the rhythm and action, then his own contribution to the dialogue can be expected. The story's momentum enables the comic teller to employ wordless passages successfully.

In the following sequence, much dialogue is suspended (in order to accelerate the narrative) and the reader is expected to supply it.

4B
4C

4B
4C

MERDE
CLIK CLIK

4B
4C

4B

SCUS...PLEASE, I'M ARMANDO LUARDI... I JUST MOVED IN NEXT DOOR...FROM ITALY!
4B

MY TELEPHONE DON'TA WORK YET! I GOTTA CALL ROME ...PLEASE CAN I USE YOURS?..UNDERSTAND, I WILL PAY YOU, OF COURSE!
ER, AH, YES, SURE.

GOTTA TELL MY WIFE, LENA, I'M ARRIVED OKAY.
OH?

HELLO, LENA, IT'S **ME**, ARMANDO...CAN YOU HEAR? YES, I'M IN AMERICA...SURE, I'M TALKING IN ENGLISH...YES, YES, TOMORROW I START IN UNCLE CARLO'S TAILOR SHOP! SURE, I'LL WRITE...NO, I'LL **TELL YOU WHEN** TO COME. CIAO, CIAO!
42

THANK YOU! HERE'S THE MONEY, GRAZI!
OKAY, SURE.

VERA, YOU CRAZY!!

I KNOW WHAT YOU THINKIN'!!

MOMMA, MOMMA LOOK AT ME... I'M FORTY YEARS OLD... I SIT HOME WITH YOU!! ALL I KNOW IS COOKING!

VERA, YOU CRAZY!!

YOU HEARD... HE'S GOT A WIFE... SO, SO HOW...?
HIS WIFE IS IN ITALY ...BUT I AM HERE...SO I WILL THINK OF A WAY!

4B
4C
WELL AHEM WHAT ER SURPRISE, MR. LUARDI... YOU ARE JUST IN TIME FOR SUPPER!

APRIL
MARCH
FEBRUARY
JANUARY
HOME SO EARLY, ARMANDO, DEAR?
COULDN'T WAIT... TONIGHT YOU'MAKIN' A NEW MEAT SAUCE!
SO... ARMANDO WHEN YOU GONNA MARRY MY VERA, EH?
MAMMA P-L-E-A-SE
4B
4C
...HELLO, LENA... ITS ME, ARMANDO...YES,YES, I KNOW...OKAY, NOW...NOW, IT'S TIME FOR YOU TO COME HERE! SURE, I'LL SEND YOU THE MONEY AND TICKETS TODAY! SURE, I LOVE YOU... I MISS YOU...
...VERA... AHEM...JUST GOTTA CALL'ER FROM MY WIFE! SHE'S COMIN' HERE TO BE WITH ME! SO,... IT'S A NO MORE FOR US!
CIAO, VERA.
NO ARMANDO... IT'S NOT FINISHED BETWEEN US!! YOU ARE MINE... I WILL FIGHT FOR YOU!!!
4C
45

4B
4B
4C
4B
4C

?!
CALENDAR
CALENDAR

7

READER INFLUENCES

No storyteller should ignore the fact that the reader has other reading experiences. Readers are exposed to other mediums, each of which has its own rhythm. There is no way of measuring it, but we know that these different media influence each other.

FILM

THE AUDIENCE IS CARRIED THROUGH THE TELLING. IT PROVIDES NO TIME FOR SAVORING PASSAGES OR CONTEMPLATION. THE VIEWER IS A SPECTATOR OF ARTIFICIAL REALITY.

TEXT

ACQUISITION REQUIRES LITERACY, WHICH INVOLVES THOUGHT, PARTICIPATION AND RECALL...READERS CONVERT WORDS INTO IMAGERY.

INTERACTIVE VIDEO

ELECTRONICALLY STORED TEXT AND IMAGERY LETS VIEWER MANIPULATE THE RHYTHM OF DISPLAY AND ACQUISITION. THERE IS NO TACTILE SENSE AS PROVIDED IN PRINT.

COMICS

ACQUISITION IS LESS DEMANDING THAN TEXT BECAUSE IMAGERY IS PROVIDED. THE QUALITY OF THE TELLING HINGES ON THE ARRANGEMENT OF TEXT AND IMAGE. THE READER IS EXPECTED TO PARTICIPATE.

READING THE IMAGERY REQUIRES EXPERIENCE AND ALLOWS ACQUISITION AT THE VIEWER'S PACE. THE READER MUST INTERNALLY PROVIDE SOUND AND ACTION IN SUPPORT OF THE IMAGES.

READING RHYTHM

Broadly speaking, and setting aside individual cognitive skills, a reader's rate of acquisition can be best described as a reading rhythm. While readers may adjust their expectations to the discipline and conventions of comics, there is a reflexive referral to other media just as there is to a memory of a real experience.

Comics' readers will tolerate the emulation of another medium's rhythm of narration, but the comic teller must deal with the fact that the medium is still delivered through print. This brings into play physical factors, i.e., paper does not require machinery for transmission. The reader is in total control of the acquisition, free of any manipulation by either the machine or the rhythm of its output.

FILM RHYTHM IN PRINT

This emulates film rhythm as its camera 'pans' or sweeps from image to image.

PRINT RHYTHM IN PRINT

In print, the rhythm of reading requires images that truly connect in order to more clearly evoke the intervening action.

THE INFLUENCE OF FILM ON READING COMICS

While there seems to be an overt relationship between comics and film, there is a substantial and underlying difference.

Both deal in words and images. Film buttresses these with sound and the illusion of real motion. Comics must allude to all of this from a platform of static print. Film employs photography and a sophisticated technology to transmit realistic images. Again, comics is limited to print. Film purports to provide a real experience, while comics narrates it. These singularities, of course, affect the approaches of the film maker and the cartoonist.

Both are storytellers working through their mediums to make contact with an audience. But each has a different engagement with its audience. Film requires nothing more than spectator attention, while comics needs a certain amount of literacy and participation. A film watcher is imprisoned until the film ends while the comics reader is free to roam, to peek at the ending, or dwell on an image and fantasize.

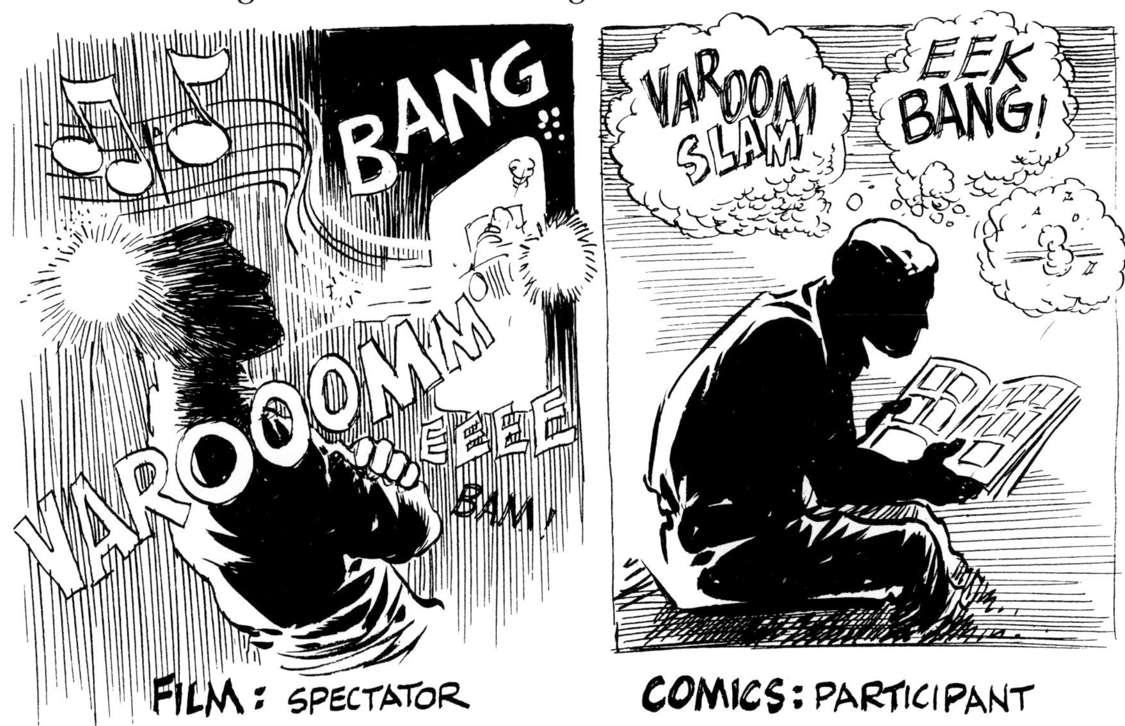

But here is where the paths really diverge. Film proceeds without any concern about the literary skills or reading ability of its audience, whereas the comic must deal with both of these. Unless comics readers can recognize the imagery or supply the necessary events that the arrangement of images imply, no communication is achieved. The comics maker is obliged, therefore, to devise images that connect with the reader's imagination.

The comic maker working in modern times must deal with a reader whose life experience includes a substantial amount of exposure to film.

Because film experience (despite the fact that it is contrived) tends to be retained, the comics narrator must deal with this experience as if it were real. It is therefore inescapable that the elements of storytelling — rhythm, problem resolution, cause and effect, as well as the more cognitive elements — relate to the reader's experience as a whole. There is an opportunity for reader contact here.

One cannot ignore the fact that the television "experience" can be aborted with the touch of a button. The influence of this on attention span and retention cannot be dismissed.

In comics, it is tempting to coopt film clichés that the cinema reader accepts viscerally. Film often uses the viewer's eye as the camera. In this device, the actors remain in position while the camera moves in and around their face or bodies. Another cliché is the presentation of what an actor sees after he is shown seeing something. Comic makers frequently are unsuccessful in emulating this because they underestimate the amount of space this requires in print.

In film, sound and dialogue do not occupy visual space, they are heard at another level. Imitating film in a comics sequence can make the sequence hard to read, as the following shows.

FILM SEQUENCE

COMICS SEQUENCE

When a comic emulates film camera technique, it can lose readability.

EMULATING FILM

THE 'READING RHYTHM' OF FILM RIDES ON A FLOW OF CONNECTED CLOSE-UPS. THIS SATISFIES THE 'MOVIE-EXPERIENCED' WITH UNDERSTOOD ACTION.

The same event can be told more frugally, leaving room for the rest of the story.

COMIC-PRINT NARRATIVE

THE 'READING RHYTHM' OF COMICS IS SLOWER BECAUSE IT INVOLVES AN INTELLECTUAL INPUT OUT OF A READER'S REAL EXPERIENCE.

HOW COMICS INFLUENCE FILM

Film makers frequently find adaptable ideas in comics. The comic teller is not working with real time or motion, so he is not restricted in any way by the reality of his images. The comic teller is free to invent and distort reality by using caricatures and devised machinery which, in reality, could not possibly work. The use of costumed heroes, acceptable in comics was the result of the innovative freedom comic tellers enjoyed because they were unfettered by the confines of the realism in live theater or film.

NATIONAL INFLUENCES

Historically, American films, with their broad international distribution, helped establish global visual and story clichés. Comics benefited and rode on their acceptance.

After World War II, each country began to develop its own cadre of comic book talent. Comic books were soon published in individual countries for indigenous populations. French, Italian, Spanish, German, Mexican, Scandinavian, Japanese and a host of other artists and writers create comics to satisfy their own readers with stories, art and icons that reflect their own national culture. This has an influence on storytelling in comics; certain stereotypical images retain a national character.

FOR EXAMPLE

There is a strong national influence on any comic teller which makes it difficult to produce images with a deliberate international intent. However, the fact that many images portray universal human posture and gesture does serve to maintain the viability of the visual language.

8

IDEAS

Most stories come from a premise. This is the basis of the contract with the reader. The following are some popular story premises.

> "WHAT IF...?" "LET ME TELL YOU ABOUT WHAT HAPPENED TO..." "NEXT, MY HERO IS THROWN INTO THIS ADVENTURE..." "HAVE YOU HEARD THE ONE ABOUT...?"

WHAT IF?

While a major element of storytelling draws on experience and reality, or the experience of it, another source centers on the fabrication of a problem.

Here are three viable premises for a story. They touch on fundamental human concerns -- fear and curiosity. In these the need to learn about how one might deal with a threat is satisfied by the manner in which the protagonist solves the problem.

For the comic teller, the "what if" formula provides a narrative with a "peg" upon which to hang a contrived sequence of events. It also offers the opportunity to fashion imagery that does not have to answer to a reality test.

The following is the opening chapter from *SIGNAL FROM SPACE* published by Kitchen Sink, 1978.

CHAPTER
1
THE SIGNAL
LIFE ON ANOTHER PLANET
BY Will Eisner

SOMETIME BETWEEN MIDNIGHT AND DAWN- ON THE MESA RADIO ASTRONOMY OBSERVATORY, NEW MEXICO...
?!
CHAK CHAK CHAK
CHAK CHAK CHAK
CRYPTO DEPT.
WAKE UP MALLEY...I HAVE SOMETHING THAT WILL BLOW YOUR MIND!
HUH?
CLIK
3

I WANT YOU TO GET INTO YOUR COMPUTER AND DECODE THESE BLIPS, NOW!!
YAWN ...THIS IS SOME KINDA CREEPY CODE!
MAN... THIS IS LIKE GIBBERISH... IT'S SIMPLE...YET, WEIRD!
AHA ...SEE? THEY'RE IN A KIND OF MODULATED SEQUENCE-OBVIOUSLY COMPRISING THE NUMBERS 1, 3, 5, 7, 11, 13, 19, 33, 29, 31... THEY CAN BE DIVIDED BY ONE.. OR BY THEMSELVES!
SO?!
SO, THIS IS A SIMPLE MATHEMATICAL TYPE CONCEPT... IT DOESN'T SAY ANYTHING! IT JUST DOES THE ARITHMETIC... OVER-AND-OVER!
WHAT'S THE MATTER ARGANO - YOU LOOK SICK!?
OH MY GOD! THAT MEANS IT'S... A SIGNAL! IT COULD ONLY HAVE A BIOLOGICAL ORIGIN...A...A FORM OF INTELLIGENCE... LIKE OUR OWN... FROM OUTER SPACE!
4/1

THIS IS A GAG! YOU GOTTA BE KIDDING!
I'LL SHOW YOU...
SEE, IT'S STILL COMING IN...
WOW!
NOW, IT'S STOPPED!
THEY'VE STOPPED SENDING! OBVIOUSLY WAITING FOR A RESPONSE!
I'LL REPORT THIS...
NO!
THINK, MALLEY... THINK!! THINK OF THE POSSIBILITIES...
LET GO!
LOOK, ARGANO- WE JUST WORK HERE... WE CAN'T CRAP AROUND!
PLEASE, MALLEY... KEEP YOUR MOUTH SHUT A FEW HOURS! I NEED A BIT OF TIME TO THINK!
5/1

WHY ARE WE GOING TO TRACKING ?
WE'VE GOT TO GET A FIX ON THE SOURCE!
TRACKING

EVENIN', I'M DR. MARK ARGANO OF MONITORING - THIS IS PROF. MALLEY OF CRYPTOLOGY... GOT A MINUTE MR. COBBS?
SURE, WHAT'S COOKING?

COULD YOU TRACK ... AND GIVE US THE SOURCE OF THIS SIGNAL?
MM... LOOKS EASY.

BASED ON STRENGTH AND FREQUENCY I FIX IT SOMEWHERE IN THIS QUADRANT! WHAT'S THE DEAL?
OH, ...ER JUST CURIOUS.
YEH, YEH!

BULL!! LET ME IN ON IT... OR NO MORE HELP FROM ME!

OKAY... OKAY... WE GOT A SIGNAL... DECODE SAYS ITS A KIND OF MESSAGE.
THERE'S AN INTELLIGENT LIFE ON ANOTHER PLANET TRYING TO REACH US.. WE NEED TO FIND THE PLANET

6/1

OKAY... HERE... I MAKE IT A PLANET OF THE STAR BERNARD, ABOUT TEN YEARS AWAY - AT CURRENT SPACE TRAVEL CAPACITY... IT'S A TINY PLANET - NOT BIGGER THAN OUR OWN MOON! ... THAT'S THE BEST I CAN DO FOR NOW.
GOOD WORK COBBS.
OKAY, NOW - WE ARE THE ONLY PEOPLE ON EARTH WHO KNOW ABOUT THIS! I WANT YOU BOTH TO SWEAR YOU'LL KEEP IT A SECRET UNTIL I CAN FIGURE OUT HOW TO CAPITALIZE ON IT!
OKAY, I SWEAR!
YEAH, SURE, WHY NOT!
WASHINGTON, D.C. 9:30 P.M. E.S.T.
COMRADE ZORKY... IT'S OUR 'MOLE' IN NEW MEXICO WITH A CODE 6... HIS NAME IS COBBS
I CAN'T TALK NOW COMRADE... I ASSURE YOU I WOULD NOT RISK THIS CALL IF IT WERE NOT VERY IMPORTANT!
CONSULATE U.S.S.R.

...YES, SIR, I'M AT HOME ALONE...I'LL WAIT HERE UNTIL YOUR LOCAL CONTACTS ME!
GAWD HE'S A SPY! 'GOOD THING WE CAME OUT HERE ARGANO!
SHH
HOLD IT!
CAREFUL, MALLEY... HE'S GOT A GUN!
YOU'RE A LOUSY COMMIE AGENT, COBBS
WE'RE GOING TO TURN YOU IN!
NOW, COOL IT... YOU GUYS HAVE BEEN SITTING ON THIS STUFF TOO LONG - THEY'LL SUSPECT YOU'RE IN IT WITH ME... SEE!
IT'S A LIE WE'RE NOT SPIES

LOOK AT IT THIS WAY... THIS IS INFORMATION THAT BELONGS TO THE WORLD -NOT FOR SOME HUSTLER ...OR ONE LOUSY CAPITALIST NATION... JUST THINK OF THE HISTORY OF MAN'S DEALINGS WITH NEW TERRITORIES... WE'RE BARBARIANS! NO, AT LEAST IF TWO MAJOR NATIONS SHARE IN IT THEY WILL HAVE SOME CHECK ON EACH OTHER!
...THIS IS A MORAL ISSUE! BESIDES - THAT SIGNAL WILL BE BEAMED AT EARTH AGAIN... THEN THE U.S. WILL HAVE IT TOO... SO, WHAT'S THE BIG DEAL?
LISTEN ARGANO... THE KGB DOESN'T YET KNOW WHAT I HAVE... SO, WHEN THEY GET HERE I'LL SHARE CREDIT WITH YOU. THEY'LL ARRANGE FOR YOU TO DEFECT TO THE U.S.S.R... YOU'LL BE A BIG SHOT THERE!
HOW ABOUT THAT?
IT STINKS COBBS ...NO!

PLEASE ARGANO, LET'S THINK IT OVER ...MAYBE WE...
NO!

THE WHOLE DEAL IS MINE! I DON'T GIVE A DAMN ABOUT ANY MORALITY CRAP!
KEEP BACK ARGANO!
THIS IS MY CHANCE TO MAKE IT BIG...
NEVER MIND LOOKIN' FOR HIS GUN-GIMME THAT ROCK, MALLEY!
HELP ME GET RID OF THIS ...UGHHH
ULKKK I'M GOING TO VOMIT
NOT HERE MALLEY-LISTEN, HE'S A LOUSY SOVIET SPY...NO BIG LOSS! THEY'LL KEEP IT HUSH-HUSH! GO HOME. TOMORROW WE'LL REPORT TO WORK LIKE NOTHING HAPPENED!

LET ME TELL YOU WHAT HAPPENED TO...

An audience is always interested in the experiences of someone with whom it can relate. There is something very private that occurs within the reader while he "shares" the actor's experience. The operative word is "share," because the inner feelings of the protagonist are understandable to the reader who would have similar emotions under the same circumstances.

In telling such a story in a graphic medium, it is necessary to establish credibility. In comics particularly, a prologue helps to invest the major character with some dimension. To do this, a prologue needs to be economical. A long prologue runs afoul of space limitations and a short one leaves the reader too much to contribute. Stories built around a protagonist often depend on a prologue to quickly introduce him.

In the following novella *"SANCTUM"* a prologue occupies the first four pages.

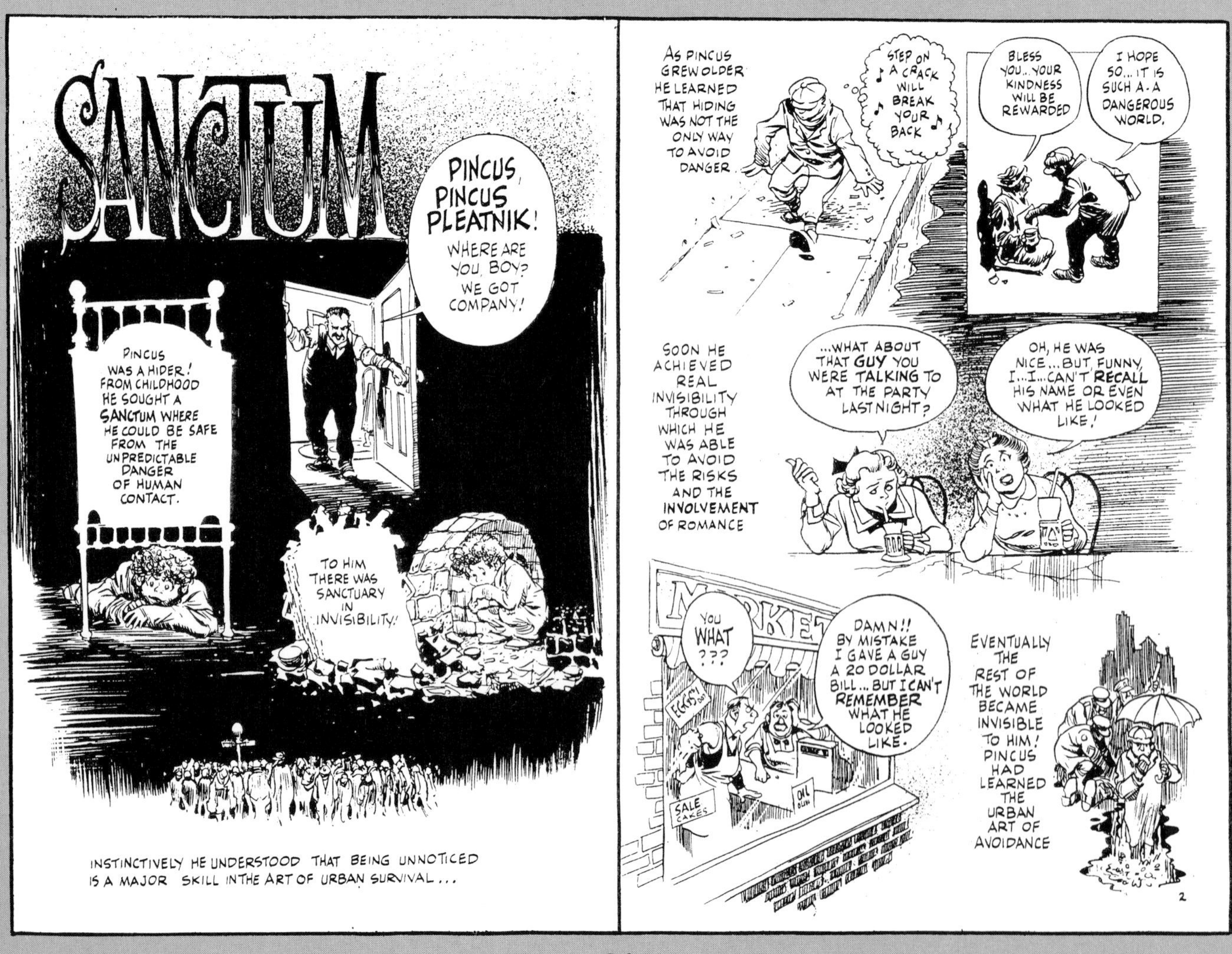

END OF PROLOGUE

JUST A MOMENT SIR... PSST.. JOE GET ME TO-DAY'S OBIT COLUMN!
NOW, SIR... YOU SAY YOU ARE PINCUS PLEATNIK? ...AH... HERE IT IS...YESS!
Pincus Pleatnik, on Friday, Nov. 14, of a stroke. At 55 Dropsie Avenue. Services at Midtown Memorial
SO, WHAT'S THE PROBLEM, SIR!?
IT'S A BIG MISTAKE I TELL YOU. ...I AM PINCUS PLEATNIK AND I AM NOT DEAD!!
NOW, NOW PLEASE CALM DOWN, MISTER! THIS DOES SAY, "Pincus Pleatnik of 55 Dropsie Ave.."
BUT I'M CALLING FROM 55 DROPSIE!!
MISTER, THERE IS NO NEED FOR HYSTERIA! WE PRINT IT AS IT IS FILED HERE!
SIR, SIR!
A NUT!
HMPF... I NEVER MAKE MISTAKES... BESIDES... MY JOB IS TO EDIT THE LISTINGS AS THEY'RE FILED WITH US... WHO DIES IS NOT MY RESPONSIBILITY!
CLIK
CLIK
CLIK
7
WHAT SHOULD I DO?
CALL THE POLICE!
WHAT FOR?
IT'S JUST A...A MISTAKE SO, WHAT COULD IT HURT?
I SHOULD CALM DOWN... BE SENSIBLE!
PINCUS...PINCUS, YOU ARE A GOOD PRESSER! YOU GOT A JOB IN ABE SHMOTTER'S STORE... YOU MAKE A LIVING!
SO, WHAT'S TO WORRY?
BESIDES, I AM A BACHELOR WITH NO KIDS...NO FAMILY! WHO WILL CARE?
IT'S MY DAY OFF... I'LL TAKE A NICE WALK IN THE PARK... MAYBE IT'LL CALM ME DOWN!
SOME NERVE ... I'VE BEEN WORKING IN OBITUARIES FOR TWENTY YEARS! I DON'T MAKE MISTAKES P-E-R-I-O-D!
CLIK
CLACK
CLIK
CLIK
8

AFTER ALL... THERE ARE LOTS OF PEOPLE WITH THE SAME NAME WHO DIE EVERY DAY!
OKAY.. SO WHAT - IF THE FUNERAL PARLOR MADE A MISTAKE IN THE ADDRESS... IS THAT MY FAULT??
I CAN ONLY PRINT WHAT THEY GIVE ME, RIGHT?
GERTIE, GET ME THE MIDTOWN MEMORIAL CHAPEL!
...I'M SORRY EDNA THEIR OFFICE IS CLOSED! IT'S FRIDAY AFTERNOON!
THANKS, GERTIE!
WELL, I TRIED... SO, WHAT AM I ...GOD??
FURNITURE 30-WEEKS TO PAY NO DOWN PAYMENT
HOLY SMOKE! HEY, CHOLLY!
9
YEH, WOT, BOSS?
DIDN'T WE DELIVER A CHIFFONIER TO A PINCUS PLEATNIK AT 55 DROPSIE?
YEAH, THREE DAYS AGO...IT'S A 20-PAYMENT DEAL!
I THOUGHT SO
PINCUS PLEATNIK DIED YESTERDAY!
REALLY? ..UH, OH!
DON'T STAND THERE, REPOSSESS THE CLOSET!!
NOW?
NOW, DUMMY! BEFORE HIS ESTATE GRABS IT!
I'M GOING, I'M GOING! IT'S FRIDAY NIGHT! I'LL BE LATE FOR SUPPER AT MY MOM'S
...BUT PINCUS PLEATNIK IS DEAD! IT'S IN THE PAPERS!!
YEAH, YOU'RE THE SUPER...Y'GOT TO LET US IN. ...WE GOT TO REPOSSESS A CLOSET!
YER SURE PINCUS IS DEAD??
I-I DON'T KNOW
HERE, LOOK AT THE PAPER!
CAREFUL, DON'T BANG UP THE WALL!
10

YES, MR SCRUGGS, I KNOW YOU ARE MY SUPER AT 55 DROPSIE! WHAT'S A MATTER ??
REAL ESTATE
ONE OF OUR TENANTS DIED?? SO??... WAS HE BEHIND IN THE RENT??... HMMMM A MONTH?.. AHA YES HE IS LISTED IN THE OBITUARY! ... PINCUS PLEATNIK!
WHADDYA MEAN ONLY ONE MONTH... HE'S BEHIND... SO, YOU KNOW WHAT TO DO! LOCK IT UP!
CHANGE THE LOCK AND PUT OUT A 'FOR RENT' SIGN... AND RAISE THE RENT!
WHADDYA MEAN WE CAN'T? ...WE GOT A LEGAL RIGHT! ... WE CAN HOLD HIS ASSETS... HE OWES US!
DON'T WORRY. I GOT LAWYERS TO HANDLE THAT! ... JUST CHANGE THE LOCK!
WHAT'S GOING ON SUPER ?
HMM IT'S 4B ...WE NEVER SEE HIM COME OR GO!
MR. PINCUS PLEATNIK DIED... I'M CHANGING THE LOCK!
11
UH, OH, IT'S GETTING LATE... TIME TO GO HOME FOR SUPPER!
HEY!!! MY DOOR IS LOCKED! MY KEY DON'T FIT!! OH... IT'S BEEN CHANGED!
WHAT'S THE BANGING OUT THERE MANNY ?
SOMEONE IS TRYING TO GET INTO PLEATNIK'S APARTMENT! ...DON'T LOOK OUT... MIND OUR OWN BUSINESS!
MR. SCRUGGS! MY DOOR IS LOCKED... I CAN'T GET IN!!
WHO YOU?
I'M PINCUS PLEATNIK OF 4B... MY DOOR IS
NAHH HE'S DEAD!
GIT OUTTA HERE... BUM!
GRRRRR!
12

HEY, CASEY! CAN YA HANDLE THIS... I'M BUSY!
SQUAD ROOM 14 PRECINCT
YEH!
MY NAME IS PINCUS PLEATNIK. I LIVE AT 55 DROPSIE ... I'VE BEEN LOCKED OUT!
YOU GOT ANY IDENTIFICATION MISTER?
YES, HERE, MY UNION CARD!
HMM SO YOU HAVE.
WHY WOULD YOU BE LOCKED OUT, NOW ?
THE SUPER THINKS I'M DEAD!
NOW, WHY WOULD HE THINK THAT ?
THE NEWSPAPER ...IN THE OBITUARY, SEE... IT'S A BIG MISTAKE!
H'LO DAILY NEWS?... THIS IS SERGEANT CASEY 14TH PRECINCT... I'M CHECKING ON AN OBITUARY... A PINCUS PLEATNIK... OH, YOU GOT A COMPLAINT FROM HIM... WELL, COULDN'T BE A MISTAK HEY!
LOOK, LADY! NO REASON TO GET SO MAD... I JUST WANT TO VERIFY YER SURE NOW? OK, OK, OK, OK, OK, G'BYE!
NOW, NOW LOOK HERE MISTER... WHY DONT CHA BE NICE AND GO HOME!? ...THERE'S A GOOD MAN!
14
14
13

I AM NOT DEAD!
TELEPHONE
14

RING RING RING RING RING RING
HAALO??
HELLO!
HELLO?! ABE SHMOTTER'S ...WHO ARE YOU? ...OH???... THE CLEANING LADY??
...WELL THIS IS PINCUS PLEATNIK! I'M THE PRESSER! ...LISTEN I MUST TALK TO—
CLICK!
TELEPHONE
15

RING RING
HELLO? YES... THIS IS MISSIS SHMOTTER. ...YES?
WHAT? WAIT, I'LL GET ABE!
OY!
REBA, LOOK AT THIS... MY PRESSER, PINCUS DIED YESTERDAY! DAMMIT!
ABE.. ABE.. YOU GOT A CALL
A CALL FOR ME..??... WHO IS IT?
IT'S THE CLEANING LADY FROM YOUR STORE, ABE!
SHE SAYS, PINCUS, YOUR PRESSER, JUST CALLED THERE AND....
HANG UP!
SURE, BUT.. BUT..
DON'T SAY ANYTHING... JUST HANG UP!!
OH, MY GOD! THEY DID IT!
WHO DID WHAT?
THAT CALL WAS THEIR WAY OF WARNING ME... THEM UNION GOONS MUSTA KILLED POOR PINCUS!
16

I DON'T UNDERSTAND, ABE...
PINCUS BELONGED TO THE MEN'S SUIT UNION... NOT THE PRESSER'S UNIOIN .. DON'T YOU SEE?
SO, HE'S UNION! WHAT'S A DIFFERENCE??
TWO LOCALS ARE FIGHTING FOR CONTROL OF MY SHOP!!
THE PRESSERS WANT TO PUT THEIR MAN INTO MY SHOP!
...I SEE... TO DO THAT THEY GOT TO MAKE A VACANCY!
OH, MY GOD!
EXACTLY!! THE DIRTY ROTTEN GOONS!
WHAT ARE YOU GOING TO DO, ABE?
...HELLO, VITO! THIS IS ABE.... OKAY, YOU WIN!! THERE'S A-A-ER VACANCY... SO, YOU CAN SEND YOUR PRESSER IN FIRST THING MONDAY!
17

MOVE ALONG, BUM.. NO LOITERING HERE.. C'MON, C'MON!
OFFICER, I'M NOT A BUM. I'M A VICTIM OF THE CITY!
MOVE!
DOES ANYONE CARE? DO YOU?
BEAT IT!
...NO!! VAGRANTS ARE A SOCIAL NUISANCE...DEBRIS... TO BE SWEPT ASIDE BY A MINDLESS AND CRUEL SYSTEM... WE ARE INVISIBLE PEOPLE!
...JUST DOING MY JOB!
HAH... YOUR JOB, YOUR JOB! WHAT ABOUT THE LIVES YOU TOUCH???!!
AAAAAH!
TO YOU IT'S JUST MOVING ONE BUM FROM A BENCH! BUT TO THE BUMS IT IS SURVIVAL!!!
?
18

WELL, LOOKEY HERE... ANOTHER PIECE OF DRIFTWOOD!
YOU, BUDDY...Y' ARE IN MY OWN PLACE... HMMM I AIN'T SEEN YOU 'ROUND HERE!
EXCUSE ME... I'VE GOT NO PLACE TO GO!
PLEASE I GOT A TEMPORARY PROBLEM! I DON'T KNOW WHERE TO GO OR WHAT TO DO ABOUT IT!
ALL OF LIFE IS TEMPORARY BUDDY! TELL ME ABOUT IT!
I'M LISTED AS DEAD IN THE OBITUARY! ...SINCE THEN I'VE BEEN LOCKED OUT IT'S LIKE I DO NOT EXIST!
HAH!! YET ANOTHER VICTIM OF THE SYSTEM!
LISTEN... I'M ONLY TRASH! I GOT NO WAY TO BEAT 'EM! BUT YOU?...YOU CAN FIGHT BACK!
YES, YES... YOU'RE RIGHT! MONDAY, FIRST THING I'LL GO TO MY JOB... I'LL PRESENT MYSELF. ...MY BOSS, ABE SHMOTTER WILL HELP ME OUT!
19

GUSSIE, DID YOU SEE THE OBITUARY IN THE PAPER FRIDAY!?
PINCUS PLEATNIK DIED! HE'S A RELATIVE, NO??
YES! ...TOO BAD!
SO?? WAS HE WORTH ANYTHING?? I MEAN WE SHOULD LOOK INTO IT, NO?
OH, HERB, THIS IS VERY EMBARRASSING! PINCUS ONLY DIED FRIDAY. ...I HARDLY EVER SAW HIM!
DON'T BE DUMB, GUSSIE! HE MAY HAVE LEFT A BUNDLE! ...YOU ARE HIS COUSIN!
VERY DISTANT... IN THE OBITUARY THEY DIDN'T EVEN MENTION MY NAME!
DID HE HAVE ANYBODY??
NO! HE WAS A SOLITARY MAN, I HEARD!
THAT IS JUST THE POINT
IF PINCUS LEFT ANY MONEY YOU SHOULD BE FIRST IN LINE!
I..I FEEL LIKE A VULTURE.
CALL OUR LAWYER!
20

YE-ES...UH HUH...YES... OKAY, GUSSIE I UNDERSTAND! NOW, THE FIRST THING WE MUST DO IS GET TO THE PINCUS' WILL... DID HE HAVE ANY MONEY!
HMMMMMM WELL HE MUST HAVE HAD A BANK ACCOUNT, A UNION PENSION... AN INSURANCE POLICY MAYBE? ANY BENEFICIARIES?? ...YOU...DON'T...KNOW?? OK,OK,OK?
IT'LL PROBABLY GO TO PROBATE...AS HIS ONLY KNOWN RELATIVE YOU SHOULD FILE NOW. ...THERE'LL BE LEGAL FEES OF COURSE!
JAKE GOLD LAW OFFICE
SO... WHAT DO WE DO NOW?
GO THRU HIS EFFECTS! HIS PAPERS ...THEY MUST BE IN HIS ROOM!
OOOH, THAT IS TOO GHOULISH FOR ME?
YOU DON'T HAVE TO! I'LL DO IT!!
I'LL BET OL' PINCUS HAD A BUNDLE STASHED AWAY!
21

A. SHMOTTER TAILORS
DING
WHO'S THERE
IT'S ME PINCUS! HAS ABE COME IN YET?
NO, HE'S COMIN' IN LATE TODAY!
FEH, FEH...I'M SOME MESS... BEEN SLEEPING IN THE PARK ALL WEEKEND! ...BOY, HAVE I GOT A PROBLEM!?
SO, WHO ARE YOU?
I'M TONY, THE PRESSER HERE.
22

WHAT PRESSER? I AM THE PRESSER HERE!
YOU?... Y'CAN'T BE... HE DIED... THE UNION SENT ME TO REPLACE HIM!
I AM NOT DEAD!
CALM DOWN! CALM DOWN! ER... I'LL BE RIGHT BACK.
HELLO... GIMME JOE, THE DELEGATE!! ... THIS IS TONY, AT SHMOTTER'S TAILOR SHOP ... YEH, YEH...
I GOT A GUY HERE WHO CLAIMS HE'S PINCUS, THEIR REGULAR PRESSER!
... WHAT? OH... HE LOOKS LIKE A... A... BUM!
LOCAL 507 NATIONAL UNION PRESSERS LOCAL 507
OKAY, TONY! NOW... JUST KEEP HIM THERE... WE'LL TAKE CARE OF IT! ...YOU GO BACK TO WORK!
HOW D'YA LIKE THAT... THE DAMN SUIT UNION SENT THEIR MAN DOWN CLAIMING HE'S A PRESSER... IT'S A MUSCLE!
WOT NERVE!
OKAY, WE'LL PLAY IT THEIR WAY... HEY, GUIDO BRING BENNO IN HERE WITCHA!
SHOO BOSS!
23

...WE GOT A LITTLE PROBLEM BOYS... GO DOWN TO SHMOTTER'S STORE AND PICK UP A GUY. ...HE'S GIVING OUR MAN, TONY, A HARD TIME!
SO, Y'WANT WE SHOULD WORK HIM OVER?
NO, NO, NO! HE'S JUST A PLANT FROM THE SUIT UNION ... A NOTHIN'
SO?
SO, WE DO A LITTLE TRICK BACK ON THEM!
JUST TAKE HIM OUT TO JERSEY... SAY, SECAUCUS... AND DROP HIM OFF OUT THERE!
NO ROUGH STUFF. ...BUT BY THE TIME HE'LL GET BACK IT'LL BE NIGHT HAW, HAW!
...BY THEN, LOCAL 406 OF THE SUIT UNION WILL GET THE MESSAGE AND LAY OFF OUR TURF!
YOU GOT IT!
YER BODDERING ME, MISTER! GO'WAY!!
THIS IS MY JOB!
24

I TELL YOU I'M THE PRESSER, HERE!
TAKE IT EASY! ...CALM DOWN. WE CAN SETTLE THIS.
WHERE IS ABE? HE'LL SETTLE IT... HE KNOWS ME AFTER ALL!
ABE IS COMIN' IN LATE, I TOLD YOU!
NOW SIT DOWN!
DING
...WHERE IS HE? OH, IS THAT HIM??
YEH!
WHO ARE YOU??
25

LET ME GO!
SHHHH
NOW, BE NICE. DON'T MAKE NO TROUBLE!
JUST STAY PUT AND SHUT UP! WE'RE JUST GOIN' FER A LITTLE RIDE!
WE DON'T WANT NO TROUBLE!
YOU DON'T EVEN KNOW WHO I AM! LET ME OUT!!
SURE WE DO!! YOU'RE A PLANT FROM LOCAL 406! NOW, SIT BACK AND YOU WON'T GET HURT!
26

YOU DON'T UNDERSTAND...I'M NOT DEAD! Y'SEE IT'S A MISTAKE!
JUST SHUT UP!
WHERE ARE YOU TAKING ME?
I TOL' YOU WE DON'T WANT NO TROUBLE!
27

HE'S NICE AND QUIET NOW.
GOOD!! KEEP HIM THAT WAY... WE'LL BE HITTING THE BACK ROADS IN A MILE OR TWO!
28

29

SCREECH
HOLY SHIT! HE JUMPED OUT ON US!!
YER GODDAM RIGHT...HE'S DEAD DOWN THERE!
WOT'LL WE DO BENNO?
KEEP OUR MOUTHS SHUT! WHO'S GONNA KNOW? LET'S GET OUTTA HERE...LET'S GET OUTTA HERE!
HIGH TIDE
30

NEXT MY HERO IS THROWN INTO THE FOLLOWING ADVENTURE

In graphic storytelling, perhaps the most comfortable format is the one in which a continuing character with well-established characteristics is plunged into a challenging adventure.

Here the comic teller need only arrange a set of "trials" for the hero. In such a story, the reader does not expect a complex plot or a tightly woven fabric of circumstances. Indeed, the simpler the problem the better. ACTION is the plot.

Such a story situation is common to super hero stories. Action serves the teller well because super heroes are one-dimensional. Given the fact that this kind of hero's attributes are essentially physical — unlimited strength, vision, locomotion, etc. — the threat can be in response to the nature of these characteristics. In this kind of story, the absence of subtlety in interaction makes for predictable plots. The comic teller can therefore resort to the novelty of movie style graphics. The movie audience develops a kind of cinematic literacy over time and will, when reading comics, often anticipate the outcome of familiar situations. By employing the images in a "special effects" style with striking camera angles the storyteller can achieve excitement within a banal plot.

"MOVIE-SHOT" IMAGES HAVE A CERTAIN STORY VALUE IN PRINT BECAUSE THEY EVOKE MOOD AND A FEELING OF ENVIRONMENT.

In the following example, the hero is not superhuman. He is established as a powerful but vulnerable fighter. The adventure into which he is thrown capitalizes on his vulnerability. The tale centers around the hero's ability to prevail.

513. Originally published March 26, 1950

THE ISLAND

CREAK

I MUST BE ON A ROLLER COASTER...

SURE... THAT'S IT! I'M IN CENTRAL CITY AND I'M RIDING ON A ROLLER COASTER...
WATER-

FOUR DAYS... FOUR DAYS!
WHAT A FOOL I WAS TO TRY TO MAKE THE MAIN-LAND WITH A WOUNDED MAN ON THIS MAKESHIFT RAFT!

NO USE, SPIRIT! YOU'VE BEEN PLUGGING AT THAT DRIED-OUT BOTTLE SINCE YESTERDAY...
...THIS IS IT...
MUM-MM-M MUMBLE
?

..SPIRIT!
IT'S LAND!
WELL, WELL, IF IT ISN'T DOLAN! HI YA, DOLAN? I'VE GOT THE JEWEL WELL-HIDDEN! NOBODY WILL EVER FIND IT...
NOBODY...
2

PUF-PUF! HE'S BURNING UP WITH FEVER! I'LL DRAG HIM HERE IN THE SHADE AND COVER HIM WITH LEAVES TO KEEP HIM WARM! PUF...

THE SUN WILL BE DOWN IN ANOTHER HALF HOUR! I'LL HAVE TO WORK FAST! I'LL BUILD A SHELTER AND START A FIRE!
RIP!

ANOTHER DESERT ISLAND! IF ONLY A SHIP WOULD COME! HOW LONG IS THIS GOING TO LAST? SPIRIT, YOU MUST GET WELL! YOU'LL BE ALL RIGHT IN A DAY OR SO! YOU WILL, DO YOU HEAR?

DARLING!

ELLEN...
ELLEN...

Later...
IT'S GETTING DARK SOONER THAN I EXPECTED! I COULDN'T HAVE BEEN GONE MORE THAN 15 MINUTES! IF ONLY THERE WAS SOME LIFE ON THESE ISLANDS? SPIRIT...I'M BACK!

HE'S GONE!
3

HEAT
SOMEWHERE ON THE ISLAND THE SPIRIT GROPES THROUGH THE JUNGLE..

BEEP A BEEP-BEEP BEEP BE

BEEP!

BEEP BEEP BEEP

BEEP BEEP BEEP BEEP
WELL, WELL, WELL, WELL, WELL!
4

BLUE MAHSK, BLUE GLAHVES... TSK, TSK... I DO BELIEVE IT'S THE **SPIRIT!**

'OW ARE YE, OL' CHAP? REMEMBER YER OL' PAL FROM CENTRAL CITY, ARCHIE FLYE? REMEMBER 'OW YE HAD ME SENT TO PRISON, F'R FORGERY?

'OW ARE YE, OLD PAL?

FLYE, TO THE SUBMARINE SNYDER... ARE YEW THEAH? STOP THOSE BLARSTED MESSAGES! NO MERCHANT SHIPS 'AVE COME BY THIS WEEK! I'LL SIGNAL WHEN THE NEXT ONE PAHSES! HOVER **AND** HOUT! KLIK!

H'I'M IN A NEW BUSINESS, **SPIRIT!** LOOK OUT FER A BAND O' SUBMARINE PIRATES! Y'PICKED A **BAD** ISLAND T' MAROON Y'SELF ON! HEH, HEH, HEH!

Meanwhile...
HE COULDN'T HAVE GONE FAR IN HIS CONDITION! **DARN THESE VINES!**

FUNNY, THE THINGS YOU SEE IN A JUNGLE! THOSE VINES LOOK ALMOST **LIKE A RADIO ANTENNA!**

HOLD THE PHONE... IT **IS** AN ANTENNA! THERE'S A RADIO STATION ON THIS ISLAND!

Meanwhile...
5

CRASH

FALL, BLAST Y'R HIDE, FALL!

THAT'LL BE ALL, MISTER... GET AWAY FROM THE SPIRIT AND PUT YOUR HANDS UP!

SPIRIT!
STAND BACK! I WARN YE... STAND BACK!
6

CLICK
CLICK

GULP
IT WAS EMPTY ALL THE TIME!

...GET A ROPE, SAND! WE'LL TIE HIM UP...
RIGHTO...AND WHILE I'M AT IT...HE'S GOT A WELL-EQUIPPED MEDICINE CHEST IN THERE! I'LL HAVE YOU TAPED UP IN A JIFFY!

Next day...
SAND...LOOK AT THIS...A MESSAGE BY RADIO JUST CAME IN...LOOKS LIKE WE ARE ON THE TRADE ROUTES, ANYHOW!
AND, IT TIES IN NEATLY! I COAXED OL' ARCHIE, HERE, INTO SHOWING ME ABOUT! THERE'S A REFUELING CACHE ON THE LEE SIDE OF THIS ISLAND...WHICH MEANS THAT PIRATE SUB SHOULD BE HERE NEXT WEEK!

That evening...
SO...ONE ADVENTURE ENDS...AND, HERE WE ARE...ON A DESERTED ISLAND FOR THE NEXT! HAH... A WHOLE WEEK, AND NOTHING TO DO BUT WAIT!
IT WON'T BE TOUGH! THERE'S PLENTY OF FOOD ON THE ISLAND!

TEE HEE! WHAT A LAUGH! 600 COLLEGE BOYS ONCE VOTED ME 'THE GIRL THEY'D LIKE TO BE MAROONED ON AN ISLAND WITH'... AND YOU... Y'BIG LUG...YOU FALL ASLEEP!

HUH...DID YOU SAY SOMETHING, SAND?
AW, SHUT UP AND GO TO SLEEP!

DID YOU HEAR THE ONE ABOUT...

Stories can be hinged on a joke. Structurally, a joke is the dramatization of a "surprise." An incongruous outcome of an act or speech, it can be either in dialogue form or presented as an incident. It is the unforeseen and unexpected which evokes the pleasure of relief or amusement that results in laughter.

In telling a joke, the teller should concentrate on staging the action or setting on which the joke depends. The reader is led up a path which veers away suddenly. While the point can be told in one or two written lines, the comic teller must flesh out a scenario that will accommodate graphics. This is done by adding background before and after the point. Vaudeville comedians called this "milking" a joke.

In this type of story, a prologue is necessary. This allows the comic teller to employ graphic devices to convey "flashback" as well as to intensify the reactions of the individuals involved. Text alone is not enough to sustain the ambiance of the graphic narrative. The telling of a joke with graphics requires that the teller maintain absolute control of the imagery. It becomes necessary, therefore, to avoid subtlety in art and to depend on stereotypes and easily recognized images.

THE STRUCTURE OF A GRAPHICALLY TOLD JOKE HAS A DEFINABLE ARCHITECTURE

In the following story, the "joke" is simple. A former hit man attempts to fulfill a contract 50 years after the date he was employed to execute it. In doing so, he dies of a heart attack. His victim survives unaware that he was about to be assassinated by a friend. The joke is in the irony of the surprising pity he feels for the hit man and the final line, "living is a risky business" is designed to make the point.

THE LONG HIT
By Will Eisner
THE BRONX...1934
HOCKIE ..NO.. ..NO..
NOTHIN' PERSONAL, AUGIE!
BANG!
SUNSHINE NEWS

...DON ANGELINO IN?? TELL HIM HOCKIE LOZANIA IS HERE TO SEE HIM!
Y'LL HAFTA WAIT... POP'S BUSY WITH SOMEBODY!
PALMA OLIVE OIL
YOU TONY, HIS KID?
YEAH
...FURTHERMORE, MR. ANGELINO-YOU CAN GO TO HELL... I'M NOT... SELLING OUT...P.E.R.I.O.D.
POP WILL SEE YOU NOW, MR. HOCKIE..
AUGIE IS ICED!
VERY GOOD, HOCKIE! I GOT ANOTHER CONTRACT FOR YOU... THIS IS A BIG ONE... FIVE THOUSAND!
WHO?
...THE GUY WHO JUST WALKED OUT!...DAVE BUNGEY...HE'S GIVIN' US TROUBLE. ...DO IT QUICK AND NEAT!
SUNSHINE NEWS

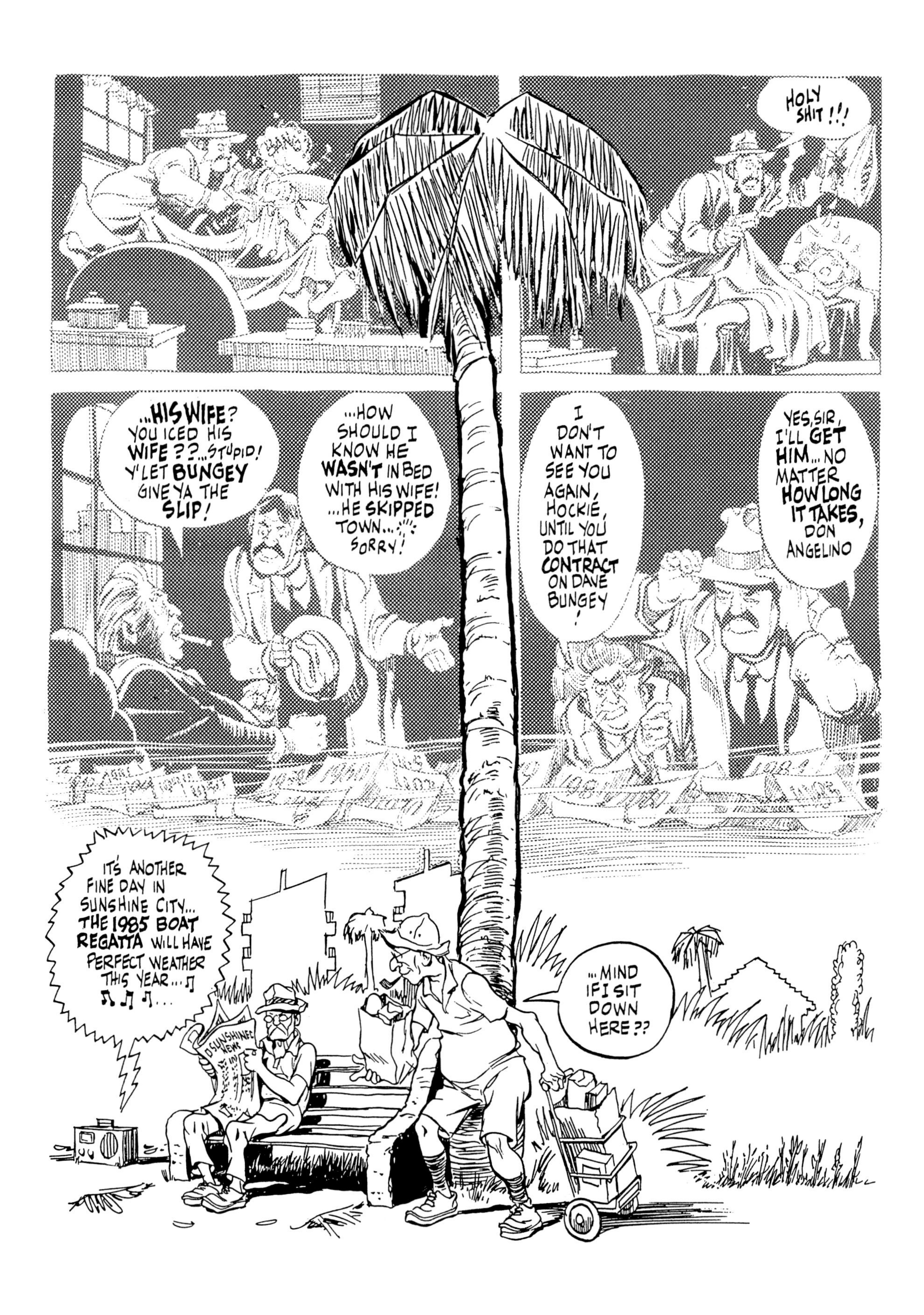
HOLY SHIT!!!
...HIS WIFE? YOU ICED HIS WIFE??...STUPID! Y'LET BUNGEY GIVE YA THE SLIP!
...HOW SHOULD I KNOW HE WASN'T IN BED WITH HIS WIFE! ...HE SKIPPED TOWN... SORRY!
I DON'T WANT TO SEE YOU AGAIN, HOCKIE, UNTIL YOU DO THAT CONTRACT ON DAVE BUNGEY!
YES, SIR, I'LL GET HIM... NO MATTER HOW LONG IT TAKES, DON ANGELINO
IT'S ANOTHER FINE DAY IN SUNSHINE CITY... THE 1985 BOAT REGATTA WILL HAVE PERFECT WEATHER THIS YEAR... ♫ ♫ ♫ ♫...
...MIND IF I SIT DOWN HERE??

:. WHEW :. IT AIN'T EASY BEIN' 83 YEARS OLD... I GET SO TIRED.
YEAH, I'M 82... AND I KNOW!

USTA BE, I WUS ABLE TO UNLOAD 200 CASES OF OLIVE OIL IN ONE AFTERNOON!
SUNSHINE NEWS

OLIVE OIL? I USTA BE IN THAT BUSINESS UP NORTH! ... WHO DID YOU WORK FOR?

PALMA OIL.. DON ANGELINO! I WAS HIS TROUBLE SHOOTER IN THEM DAYS ... YOU KNOW, LABOR PROBLEMS AND SUCH!
HIM? OH, HA, HA, THAT OLD MAFIOSO ... BOY, HE WAS SOME GONNIF!
SUNSHINE NEWS

LEMME TELL YOU ... ONE TIME HE TRIED TO RUB ME OUT!! BUT THE BASTARD KILLED MY WIFE BY MISTAKE .. BUT I GOT AWAY...CAME SOUTH ... NOW, I HEAR HIS SON, TONY, TOOK OVER WHEN HE DIED....

WHAT'S YOUR NAME?
DAVE BUNGEY ... WHAT'S YOURS?

HENRY LOZANIA ... CALL ME 'HOCKIE'
PLEASED TO MEET YOU!

LIKEWISE, I'M SURE!

PALMA INTERNATIO
MR. ANGELINO, A MR. HOCKIE IS ON THE PHONE ... HE SAYS IT'S URGENT!
WHO?
...YES... THIS IS TONY... MY FATHER DIED 30 YEARS AGO! ..WELL...I SORT OF REMEMBER YOU!!
CONTRACT, ... WHAT CONTRACT ??
LOOK, HERE, MY GOOD MAN... IF YOU DID HAVE A CONTRACT WITH MY FATHER WE HAVE NO RECORD!...EH? IT'S ORAL??... EXACTLY WHAT WERE THE TERMS?. WE CAN'T HONOR THIS KIND OF THING!!
LISTEN KID— I HAVE A CONTRACT WITH ANGELINO UNTIL 'NO-MATTER-WHEN'!! HE WAS A MAN OF HONOR!
$5000 FOR A HIT... AND YOU KNOW WHAT I MEAN, TONY !!
I PROMISED TO TAKE CARE OF DAVE BUNGEY AND NOW I FOUND HIM, SEE... HOCKIE LOZANIA ALWAYS DELIVERS... YOU'LL HEAR FROM ME SOON!

MONDAY
...I ENJOY PLAYIN' GOLF WITH YA, HOCKIE, BUT YOU'RE TOO SLOW...Y'KEEP LAGGIN' BEHIND!
GO AHEAD DAVE I'LL 'ER' CATCH UP!
CLICK
DAMN!! ..RUSTY OLD ROD!
CLICK
CLICK
HEY, HOCKIE, WOT'S KEEPIN' YOU?
TUESDAY
HI DAVE...I, AH. HEARD ABOUT YOUR ACCIDENT... -YOU OKAY?
SURE... JUST A LITTLE SHOOK UP...THE MECHANIC MUSTA GOOFED! MY BRAKE LINES WERE DISCONNECTED.
HAH!! THEM YOUNG MECHANICS, WHAT DO THEY KNOW !!
YOU DON'T LOOK SO GOOD YOURSELF, HOCKIE!

A WEEK LATER
... SURE IS GOOD TO BE UP AND AROUND AGAIN, HOCKIE... AHH.. WHAT'S THIS?... JELLY? GREAT... MY FAVORITE...
MY PLEASURE, DAVE.
...HELLO, HOCKIE... DON'T EAT THAT JELLY... I GAVE A JELLY CRACKER TO MISSIS GOODMIN'S CAT... AND IT GOT SICK AND DIED!!
...THANKS, DAVE..... THANKS
...AND THE FOLLOWING WEEK
HELLO! GET ME MR. TONY ANGELINO... I GOT GOOD NEWS!!

WADDYA MEAN HE'S NOT IN TO ME !? THIS IS HOCKIE !
YOU TELL HIM I DID IT !!
DAVE IS AS GOOD AS DEAD
OH
NICE FUNERAL ...TOO BAD... POOR HOCKIE. NOT MANY CAME...
FUNERAL HOME
WAS HE A GOOD FRIEND OF YOURS, DAVE?
...WELL, NOT REALLY! I DIDN'T KNOW MUCH ABOUT HIM... WE USTA BE IN THE SAME BUSINESS YEARS AGO...
OH BOY... WHAT A ROUGH COUPLA WEEKS... FIRST, I HAVE A CAR ACCIDENT... THEN, THAT POISON JELLY... AND YESTERDAY THERE'S A HOT WIRE IN MY BATH TUB... I COULDA BEEN ELECTROCUTED... AND LAST NIGHT HOCKIE DIES OF A CARDIAC ARREST.'
WHEW... LIVING IS A RISKY BUSINESS..!! EH, DAVE?

THE WRITING PROCESS

Writing is commonly perceived as confined to the manipulation of words. The process of writing for graphic narration concerns itself with the development of the concept, then the description of it and the construction of the narrative chain in order to translate it into imagery. The dialogue supports the imagery — both are in service to the story. They combine and emerge as a seamless whole. The *ideal* writing process occurs where the writer and artist are the same person. This, in effect, *shortens* the distance between the idea and its translation. It produces a product that more closely reflects the intent of the writer.

In theater or film, the script falls into the hands of directors, actors, cameramen and other technicians. In comics, the writing will be "broken down" into panels and pages by one or more artists. In some cases a "breakdown" or roughly sketched interpretation acts as a blueprint.

There is a distinct difference between writing for a book of text and a graphic novel. For one thing, a type font has no involvement in the nature, structure or quality of a story. Type does not translate; images do.

Writing that is translated into graphic dramatization, whether film or comics, must adapt to the mechanics of the form. For example, writing for film or comics is economical, eschews literary style, and does not need descriptive passages that evoke images by analogous prose. The *idea* is the dominant element. Often a writer will reinforce the translation process by supplying "depth" descriptions not intended to be reproduced, but rather designed to give the artist guidance.

In effect, writing in the graphic medium means writing for the artist. The writer supplies the concept, plot and cast of characters. His dialogue (balloons) is addressed to the reader, but the description of the action is addressed to the graphic translator.

WRITER VS. GRAPHIC TRANSLATOR

A script for comics that describes the psychological nuances of a character does so with the hope that the artwork will adequately convey such internalization.

Here, for example, is the task facing a translating artist who must deal with the following script (panel one, page one) of a 10-page high action crime story built mainly on pursuit.

Panel One

Scene

The detective enters from the left. He limps a bit (an old war wound) and favors the leg. His craggy face is a tale of years of struggle, pain and disappointment. His eyes are cold blue steel and with a swift jungle animal scan, they sweep the room. This man has killed. He is seething with rage at the humiliation of being called in so late to the case. He masks his anger but not his twitching jaw muscles.

Show middle distance shot slightly from above with Commissioner and other officers standing awkwardly against the office wall.

Balloon:

Dick: WELL SIR I GOT YOUR CALL. IF YOU EXPECT ME TO TIDY UP A MESS, YOU'D BETTER PUT THOSE CLERKS INTO STORAGE

Commish: NOW DICK, THIS IS A VERY TOUCHY SITUATION.

The script provides the artist with an internal view of the detective in the hope that the character can be limned well enough to imply all that the writer hopes to convey. But we know that to portray things like "an old war wound," "eyes sweeping the room," "seething rage," "humiliation," "working jaw muscles" may not be possible in a single middle-shot panel.

What is the writer asking for? Is the writer willing to permit these characteristics to be "divined" by the reader, or is it critical to the story that they be clearly shown?

The artist is faced with a translation dilemma. How important is the "twitching jaw muscles" and the other subtle characteristics? Indeed, how much needs to be shown in one panel? It is, of course, possible to ultimately convey the detective's persona by small inferences in successive panels, providing that fast-paced action does not interfere. Another accommodation is to insert a narrative panel that shows the subtle sub-surface characteristics. All of this depends on space.

As this example demonstrates, graphic narrative writing must deal with the limitations of the medium as well as the interpretation of the artist.

THIS ADHERES TO THE SCRIPT BUT IT OBVIOUSLY CANNOT CLEARLY DELIVER THE NUANCES REQUIRED

IF THE HERO'S PERSONALITY IS CRITICAL TO THE PLOT—IT CAN BE DELIVERED BY ADDING PANELS

Comics is a medium confined to still images, bereft of sound and motion, and writing must accommodate these restrictions.

Writers must also factor into their expectations the skills of the artist. The artist or the writer (or both) are challenged by the need to convey "internals." Subtle gestures or provocative postures are not easy to depict without the continuing movement afforded by film. In this medium "telling" images must be extracted from the flow of action and then frozen.

Another example of writing that runs afoul of the medium's limitations is the following passage:

> "The detective dropped gracefully through the manhole into a space between the crates of ammunition. He would wait there until the killers brought their prisoner into a space lit by an anemic 40-watt bulb at the end of the room.
>
> "His mind rewound. It was Vietnam again. The Delta was still. He was wondering whether the beating of his heart could be heard as he waited behind the boxes of 50-caliber rounds. The months of basic back at Parris Island really hadn't prepared him for this. Ah yes, in the barrio — where he misspent his preschool years — was more like it. His 'big brother' taught him well. 'Paulo, when you drop from the fire escape, freeze. Do not even wiggle your ass. You stay in the alley behind the garbage can until they come into the light. Those T-bones, they can smell you.'
>
> The door's slam wiped out his reverie. Suddenly he was alert. He peered around the box ready to spring. Then, the cold steel mouth of an automatic pressing against the nape of his neck brought him slowly upright."

For the storyteller to translate this narrative to graphics, a decision about how to deal with the flashback must be made during the *breakdown* stage. The writer must know that to show a replay of memory will require space. Flashbacks can also slow the action. In this case, the amount of space, allocated in the breakdown, will determine how much narrative to eliminate.

Imagine for this purpose you are the artist and you must translate this passage into a graphic narrative: How many panels would you devote to paragraph one? Yes, it would be easy to show the detective dropping through the manhole — but how would you convey the idea that he was going down to await the killers and their prisoner? How many panels would you devote to this?

In the second paragraph, the reader is invited to tour the man's past. There's a lot of story here. How do you keep it from slowing the action — that is, keep the story flow alive? The third paragraph is a problem in posture and gesture.

There are instances where narrative text is integral to the graphic. In such a case, the art becomes only an illustration in support of the text. Here is an example of a fantasy story in which text carries the "flashback." In doing so it becomes integral to the method of narration.

THE TRIAL
IN 1916 A TRIAL WAS HELD IN THE MIND OF FRANZ KAFKA
THE CZECH AUTHOR, A GOVERNMENT WORKER WITH A JURISPRUDENCE DEGREE, REALLY NEVER INTENDED THE CASE TO BE CONCLUDED.
THE ACCUSED ('K'), A BANK CLERK, FINDS HIMSELF THE SUBJECT OF UNDEFINED CHARGES. HIS STRUGGLE WITH THE INVISIBLE WEB SPUN BY NEVER-CLEARLY DEFINED AUTHORITIES HAS MADE THIS AN ENDURING CLASSIC. IT PRESAGES THE DILEMMA OF MODERN-DAY CITIZENS LIVING IN A SOCIETY OF COMPLEX LAWS AND IRON BUREAUCRACY.
* Kafka died in 1924. He left firm instructions that this and other works be "burned unread".

THE APPEAL
BY Will Eisner
NEW YEAR 86
AHA... THE DEFENDANT HAS ARRIVED AT LAST!
WHAT IS THIS?

WHO ARE YOU? THIS IS MY ROOM! HOW DID YOU GET IN HERE?
PLEASE... CONDUCT YOURSELF IN A VERY CIVILIZED MANNER! WE ARE TRYING TO PROCEED WITH A TRIAL HERE

AHEM ... THE APPELLATE BRANCH OF THE TENTH COURT OF PRAGUE IS IN SESSION... THE PLAINTIFF IS MR. K ... THE OTHERS ARE THE JURY!
THIS IS ABSURD. WHO ARE YOU?

I AM THE ATTORNEY FOR THE PLAINTIFF.

MR. K... WILL YOU GIVE SWORN TESTIMONY ?
YES.
MY GOD... THIS MAN IS... ...HE'S BEEN STABBED HE'S....

PRECISELY!... IT IS THE BASIS OF MY CLIENT'S COMPLAINT...BUT, THAT IS SPECIFIED IN THE CHARGES!

I CAN'T BELIEVE THIS !
NOW, PLEASE, REMOVE YOUR COAT, COME NOW, WE HAVE A LONG TRIAL AHEAD!

AHEM!
LISTEN, MY NAME IS...
QUIET! IT'S IRRELEVANT. IN 1916 YOU WERE A MEMBER OF THE COURT THAT BROUGHT A CHARGE AGAINST MY CLIENT, MR. K

PLEASE, MR. K... TELL US IN YOUR OWN WORDS
WELL, ONE MORNING IN MY ROOM I RANG FOR BREAK-FAST...

INSTEAD... AN OFFICIAL ENTERED MY ROOM!
...HE ORDERED ME TO DRESS AND GO TO THE NEXT ROOM AT ONCE.
THERE SAT THE INSPECTOR WHO, WHILE EATING MY BREAKFAST, ANNOUNCED THAT I WAS UNDER ARREST!

...DESPITE THE FACT THAT NO SPECIFIC CHARGES WERE LEVELED THE FOLLOWING EVENTS PROCEEDED IN AN INEXORABLE SEQUENCE.
FIRST... MY AFFAIR WITH FRAULEIN BÜRSTNER SOURED. ...WHILE SHE BELIEVED ME QUITE INNOCENT, IT WAS CLEAR THAT SHE HAD LOST SOME INTEREST IN ME...
THE NEXT WEEK I RECEIVED A PHONE CALL THAT ADVISED ME A COURT OF INQUIRY WOULD CONVENE AT A HOUSE IN JULIUSSTRASSE! I WAS URGED TO ATTEND! ...OF COURSE I WENT!

THE EXAMINATION WAS WITHOUT ANY SUBSTANCE
"Are you a house painter?" ASKED THE CHIEF MAGISTRATE
"No, I'm a bank clerk," I ANSWERED FIRMLY
WHEREUPON I DELIVERED AN AGGRESSIVE REVIEW OF MY SITUATION... I SAID THAT I WAS ARRESTED IN MY ROOM, FOLLOWING WHICH MY INTERROGATOR (WHILE HE ATE MY BREAKFAST) INFORMED ME THAT I WAS UNDER ARREST! WHEN I ASKED WHAT THE CHARGE WAS, HE GAVE ME SILENCE.. NO ANSWER!
I DEMANDED TO BE GIVEN THE CHARGE AT ONCE!
THE RESPONSE WAS LAUGHTER... AND I LEFT WITHOUT SATISFACTION.

WELL, THE MATTER WAS FAR FROM CLOSED, I CAN TELL YOU... WHEN ONE HAS A CHARGE LEVELED AGAINST HIM IT CAN BE QUITE A BURDEN... MY WORK AT THE BANK WAS SUFFERING... I HAD NO CHOICE BUT TO CONFRONT IT...
I WENT TO MY UNCLE KARL. HE FEARED THAT THE FAMILY WOULD BECOME INVOLVED. THIS LED HIM TO SECURE FOR ME A LAWYER, NAMED FULD WHO WAS, HIMSELF, QUITE SICK... BUT IT WAS HIS WOMAN AIDE (LENI) WHO ADVISED ME THAT UNLESS I WOULD PLEAD GUILTY - THEY COULD NOT HELP... I REFUSED!
I TRIED ALL AVENUES... I APPEALED TO THE PAINTER WHO HAD A STUDIO BEHIND WHICH WAS THE COURT.... TO NO AVAIL! NEXT, I DISMISSED MY LAWYER AND APPLIED TO A MR. BLOCK WHO ADVISED ME AGAINST ANY INDEPENDENT ACTION. FINALLY.... I MET WITH A PRIEST... A FUTILE MEETING! IN THE END, NEITHER MY INNOCENCE NOR GUILT WAS RESOLVED.
FINALLY... ON THE EVE OF MY 31ST BIRTHDAY... AT ABOUT NINE P.M., I RECEIVED TWO VISITORS
"Good evening, Herr K," THEY SAID!
"So, you have come for me?" I ANSWERED.

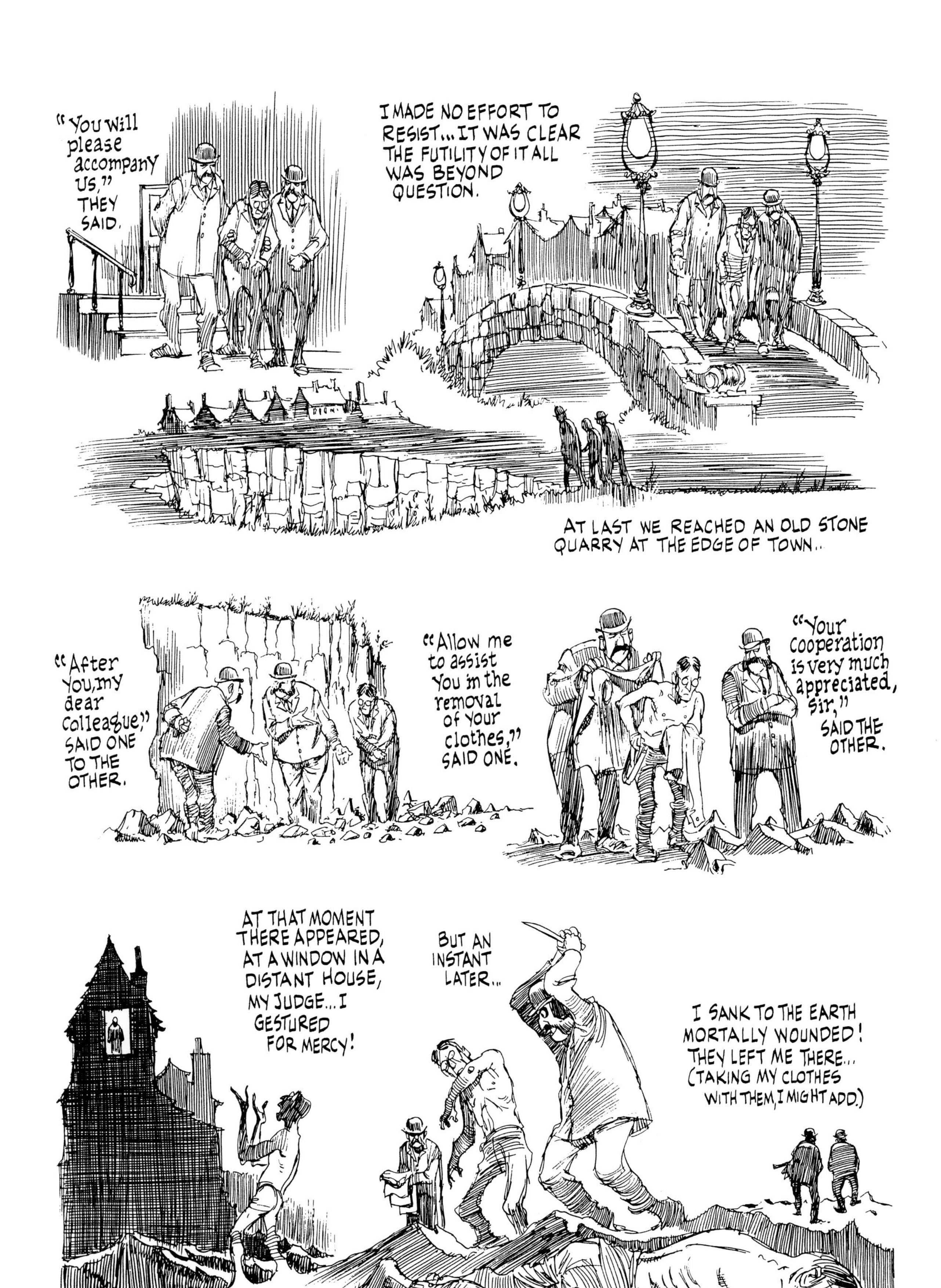
"You will please accompany us," THEY SAID.
I MADE NO EFFORT TO RESIST... IT WAS CLEAR THE FUTILITY OF IT ALL WAS BEYOND QUESTION.
AT LAST WE REACHED AN OLD STONE QUARRY AT THE EDGE OF TOWN..
"After you, my dear colleague," SAID ONE TO THE OTHER.
"Allow me to assist you in the removal of your clothes," SAID ONE.
"Your cooperation is very much appreciated, sir," SAID THE OTHER.
AT THAT MOMENT THERE APPEARED, AT A WINDOW IN A DISTANT HOUSE, MY JUDGE... I GESTURED FOR MERCY!
BUT AN INSTANT LATER...
I SANK TO THE EARTH MORTALLY WOUNDED! THEY LEFT ME THERE... (TAKING MY CLOTHES WITH THEM, I MIGHT ADD.)

SO,...YOU WERE DISPATCHED...LIKE A DOG...WHO WAS THE MAN IN THE WINDOW?
HIM!

ME?? I WAS ONLY AN OBSERVER...TRUE, I WAS THE JUDGE, BUT I NEVER 'HEARD' THE CASE
SILENCE! THE EVIDENCE IS CLEAR. BESIDES, WE HAVE THE WORD... OF THE VICTIM...

GENTLEMEN, HAVING HEARD THE TESTIMONY OF THE PLAINTIFF... HOW DO YOU FIND?
GUILTY!
GUILTY!

FOR THE CRIME OF PREMEDITATED SILENCE IN THE TRIAL OF K...AND HIS EXECUTION, THIS COURT FINDS YOU GUILTY IN THE FIRST DEGREE!
NO, NO.

...AND WE SENTENCE YOU TO ASSUME RESPONSIBILITY FOR THE PLAINTIFF...SHELTERING HIM UNTIL YOUR NATURAL DEATH!

WAIT!
GOOD DAY!
I'M TIRED, PLEASE... DO YOU MIND IF I LIE DOWN HERE ON YOUR BED?
YOU CAN'T DO THIS TO ME ...I'M NOT GUILTY.
PLEASE... ACCEPT THEIR VERDICT... THERE IS LITTLE YOU CAN DO ABOUT IT!!
THIS IS AMERICA, 1986... I CAN ASSURE YOU, I SHALL APPLY TO THE POLICE.
DON'T BE A FOOL. HOW WOULD YOU BE ABLE TO EXPLAIN A DEAD MAN IN YOUR ROOM?.. CLEARLY, SIR, YOU ARE MY PRISONER!
Help!! I am a prisoner

AFTERWORD ON WRITING

Not surprisingly, there often are communication problems between participants in the process of graphic storytelling.

In writing for graphic storytelling, the ultimate judgment of the narrative is made after the work is translated into art. The writer, therefore must be aware of the obstacles on the way to publication.

When text alone is the vehicle in conveying a story to the reader, there is little chance of a misperception. But from text to visual, there is a high probability of a difference in outcome, stemming from lack of skill to lack of time. In this medium, storytelling is not always a straight line from the mind to the reader. Here is what often happens.

10

STORYTELLERS

In the comics medium, the continuing adventure narrative first appeared in the daily newspaper strips. This was feasible because until the 1930s, newspapers dominated popular reading and were a regular uninterrupted family companion. In those years, there was fierce competition on the newsstands and comics, particularly continuity strips, held the loyalty of readers. This required storytelling skills.

In 1934, Milton Caniff (in those days most cartoonists wrote and drew their own strips) began *Terry and the Pirates.* This strip went beyond the daily joke format and purported to be a never-ending story. Caniff was carrying forward the "adventure" theme that Lyman Young began in *Tim Tyler's Luck* a few years previous. Caniff not only brought sophisticated art to the medium but his storytelling, albeit parsed out daily in segments, was so sturdy that it was usable material for the aborning comic books.

In his book, *The Art of The Funnies,* R.C. Harvey credits Caniff with "virtually redefining the adventure strip by infusing exotic tales with palpable realism. As a storyteller he enhanced the traditional formula by incorporating character development into action-packed plots."

The introductory strip for *Terry and The Pirates* (1934) laid out the cast of characters and set the story track. In later sequences (1935), Caniff demonstrates his brilliant control of storytelling. Remember, a full day elapsed between each strip, yet he never lost his readers.

AUNT AUGUSTA - THIS IS MR PAT RYAN, MR TERRY LEE AND THEIR SERVANT, CONNIE!
WHAT? INTRODUCING ME TO A SERVANT?
MISS NORMANDIE IS VERY WEAK, MRS DRAKE - YOU MUSTN'T EXCITE HER!
AND WHO AH YOU TO DICTATE TO ME SUH?
THAT DOESN'T MATTER - THE POINT IS - SHE MUST BE KEPT QUIET!
THEN IT WOULD SEEM ADVISABLE FOAH YOU AHND YOAH RAGAMUFFIN CREW TO GO AWAY!
YOU'RE RIGHT! IT'S HIGHLY ADVISABLE!
PAT!
TUT TUT DAHLING! SUCH PEOPLE MUST BE KEPT IN THEAH PLACES!
MILTON CANIFF
12-2

WELL, WHY AH YOU STANDING THEAH? IF YOU WISH TO LEAVE YOU MAY DO SO!
MADAM, WE WOULDN'T DISPLEASE FOR ANYTHING!
12-3

PAT, DARLING! DON'T LEAVE ME!
WE SEEM TO ANNOY YOUR AUNT AUGUSTA - I THINK IT'S BETTER FOR US TO GO!

WISELY SPOKEN, YOUNG MAN - IF YOU EXPECT SOME COMPENSATION FOAH YOAH EFFORTS MR. DRAKE WILL REIMBURSE YOU!
MILTON CANIFF

WHY..
HOLD IT, PAT! WE WANT NO MONEY, MRS DRAKE! SINCE YOU DON'T SEEM TO LIKE US WE'LL TAKE CARE TO KEEP OUT OF YOUR WAY!
HMPH!

LATER, IN MR. AND MRS. DRAKE'S ROOM IN THE BRITISH COMMANDANT'S HOUSE
NORMANDIE WAS PRETTY BROKEN UP BY THE WAY YOU TREATED YOUNG RYAN, GUSSIE!
OF CAWSE! I FULLY EXPECTED HER TO BE! AND DON'T CALL ME GUSSIE!
12-4

BUT, AUGUSTA, THOSE YOUNG PEOPLE ARE IN LOVE! CAN'T YOU SEE THAT?
VEDDY CLEAHLY, MY DEAH!
MILTON CANIFF

I ADMIRE YOUNG RYAN - AND I THINK HE'D BE AN IDEAL HUSBAND FOR NORMANDIE!
YOU WOULD!!

— WHY DID YOU DRIVE HIM AND THE BOYS AWAY? DON'T YOU KNOW HE'LL RUSH BACK TO TELL HER HE LOVES HER IN SPITE OF YOU?
WHICH IS EXACTLY WHAT I WANT HIM TO DO!

REGARDLESS OF YOUR HIDE BOUND SOCIAL DOCTRINES, I THINK YOU WILL BE DOING A GREAT WRONG IF YOU INTERFERE WITH NORMANDIE'S HAPPINESS!
I AM THE BEST JUDGE OF THAT!
12-5

THIS DINNER WITH THE COMMANDANT WOULD BORE ME - YOU GO AHEAD - TELL HIM I HAVE A HEADACHE!
AS YOU WISH, MY DEAR!

AFTER MR DRAKE HAS GONE, MRS DRAKE WALKS SWIFTLY TO THE DOCK WHERE THEIR CHARTERED BOAT IS MOORED
— YOU UNDUHSTAND YOAH ORDUHS, CAPTAIN?
YES, MADAME!
MILTON CANIFF

HAVE STEAM UP IN THE SHIP - AND WHEN THE LIGHT FLASHES IN THE WINDOW MY MEN COME TO THE HOSPITAL WITH A STRETCHER!
RIGHT! AND HEAH'S A HUNDRED DOLLAHS FOAH YOAH TROUBLE!

IS THE COAST CLEAR, DARLIN?
YES - UNCLE CHAUNCEY AND AUNT AUGUSTA ARE HAVING DINNER WITH THE POST COMMANDER!
12-6
IT WAS AWFUL THE WAY SHE TREATED YOU AND THE BOYS! I'M SORRY!
WE CAN TAKE IT SWEET LADY!
OH PAT - WHAT ARE WE GOING TO DO? I LOVE YOU SO -
IT'S ALL SETTLED
MILTON CANIFF
WHAT DO YOU MEAN?
YOU'RE GOING TO MARRY ME - HEAVEN HELP YOU - WHETHER YOU LIKE IT OR NOT!

WHY MISTER RYAN! I THOUGHT A MAN ALWAYS ASKED A GIRL TO MARRY HIM!
ALL RIGHT, IF YOU WANT TO BE SO TECHNICAL I'M ASKING YOU!!
12-7
AND I'M SAYING YES! - WITH ALL MY HEART!
DARLIN'!
IT'LL BE A TOUGH LIFE! NO SOCIAL REGISTER STUFF! YOU'LL BE LUCKY IF YOU EAT REGULARLY!
OH, I DON'T CARE IF WE PAT!
MILTON CANIFF

AUNT AUGUSTA!!
12-9
IT SEEMS I ARRIVED AT A MOST DRAMATIC MOMENT!
WHY-AH, MRS. DRAKE...
YOU MIGHT AS WELL KNOW THAT I HAVE ASKED NORMANDIE TO MARRY ME - AND SHE HAS ACCEPTED!
I SUSPECTED AS MUCH...
MILTON CANIFF
... AND ALTHOUGH YOU HAVE NOT ASKED IT - I GIVE MY CONSENT, AND MY BLESSING TO YOU BOTH!
Reg. U. S. Pat. Off.
Copyright, 1935, by Chicago Tribune-N. Y. News Syndicate, Inc.

AUNTIE! YOU-YOU- MEAN YOU DON'T MIND IF WE GET MARRIED?
NO, MY DEAH! - YOU HAVE MY PERMISSION - AND MY BLESSING!
12-10
WHY, MRS. DRAKE! - I - YOU - AH - THANK YOU!
OH, AUNT AUGUSTA! - WE'RE SO GRATEFUL!
BUT AUNTIE - WHY WERE YOU SO RUDE TO PAT WHEN YOU ARRIVED?
ONE MUST BE VEDDY CAREFUL, DAHLING! - SINCE THEN YOAH UNCLE HAS TOLD ME WHAT A SPLENDID YOUNG MAN MR. RYAN REALLY IS!
YOU'RE SWELL, MRS. DRAKE! - I'M SORRY - I MISJUDGED YOU BEFORE!
WE WERE BOTH EXCITED! - YOU MUST GO NOW! NAWMANDIE MUST HAVE HER REST!
MILTON CANIFF
Reg. U. S. Pat. Off.
Copyright, 1935, by Chicago Tribune-N. Y. News Syndicate, Inc.

OH, AUNTIE—I WAS SURE YOU'D LIKE PAT WHEN YOU KNEW HIM BETTER! —YOU'VE BEEN SO KIND TO US!
NOTHING AT ALL MY DEAH! —I ALWAYS HAVE YOAH BEST INTERESTS AT HAHT!
I'M SO HAPPY I COULD CRY!
12-11

THIS NERVOUS STRAIN IS NOT GOOD FOAH YOU, DAHLING! —I'VE PREPAHED A STRONG SLEEPING POTION SO YOU WILL REST BETTAH! —DRINK THIS DOWN!

SHORTLY NORMANDIE DROPS OFF INTO A DEEP SLUMBER... MRS. DRAKE WAITS A FEW MOMENTS, THEN....
... SHE CARRIES THE LAMP TO THE HOSPITAL WINDOW....
THAT'S TH' SIGNAL, MEN! LET'S GO!
MILTON CANIFF

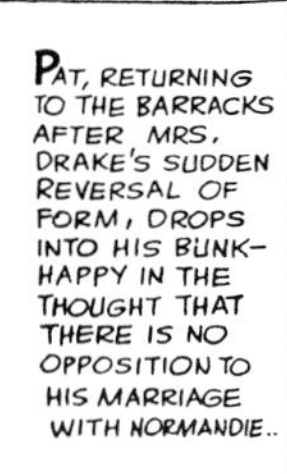
PAT, RETURNING TO THE BARRACKS AFTER MRS. DRAKE'S SUDDEN REVERSAL OF FORM, DROPS INTO HIS BUNK—HAPPY IN THE THOUGHT THAT THERE IS NO OPPOSITION TO HIS MARRIAGE WITH NORMANDIE..
12-12

OH BOY! —AND TO THINK I HATED HER WHEN I FIRST SAW HER! —NOW OL' FOOTLOOSE RYAN IS ABOUT TO PULL ON TH' CARPET SLIPPERS FOR KEEPS!

...TOUGH ON TERRY AN' CONNIE, IN A WAY—BUT WE CAN FIX THAT! —IT'S TH' QUIET LIFE FOR—ME FROM—NOW-----

FOR HOURS PAT SLEEPS SOUNDLY—THEN HE AWAKENS WITH A VIOLENT START....
WOW! —WHAT A NIGHTMARE! —I'D SWEAR I HEARD NORMANDIE CALLING ME! —SEEMS SILLY—BUT I THINK I'LL RUN OVER AN' SEE IF SHE'S OKAY...
MILTON CANIFF

DRESSING HURRIEDLY, PAT RUSHES TO THE HOSPITAL....THE SLEEPY ATTENDANT GREETS HIM....
—OH! —HIT'S YOU, MISTER RYAN! —HI THOUGHT YOU'D GONE!
12-13

WHY SHOULD I BE GONE? —I WANT TO KNOW IF MISS DRAKE'S ALL RIGHT!
WHY, BLIGH'ME, MISTER RYAN —SHE MUST BE ALL RIGHT!
MILTON CANIFF

WHAT DO YOU MEAN, MUST? —DON'T YOU KNOW?
'OW COULD HI, SIR?..

.. MRS. DRAKE AN' SOME MEN FROM THEIR SHIP CAME AN TOOK 'ER! —THEY SAILED FOR TH COAST HOURS AGO!

NORMANDIE GONE? —WHERE'S THE DOCTOR? WHERE IS HE?
IN 'ERE, SIR!
12-14

DOCTOR! THIS MAN TELLS ME MRS. DRAKE TOOK NORMANDIE TO THEIR SHIP AND SAILED FOR THE COAST! —IT CAN'T BE TRUE!
BUT IT IS, RYAN!

I WROTE A HOSPITAL DISCHARGE FOR THE GIRL, AND MRS. DRAKE HAD HER REMOVED TO THEIR PRIVATE BOAT WHILE SHE SLEPT! —I SUPPOSED YOU WENT ALONG!
BUT MR. DRAKE—DID HE GO TOO?

—COME TO THINK OF IT, I DIDN'T SEE HIM AROUND AT THE TIME! —MAYBE HE'S IN HIS ROOM!
BLIGH'ME, SIR! —RYAN LEFT LIKE A FLASH! —HI B'LIEVES 'E'S A BIT UPSET!
MILTON CANIFF

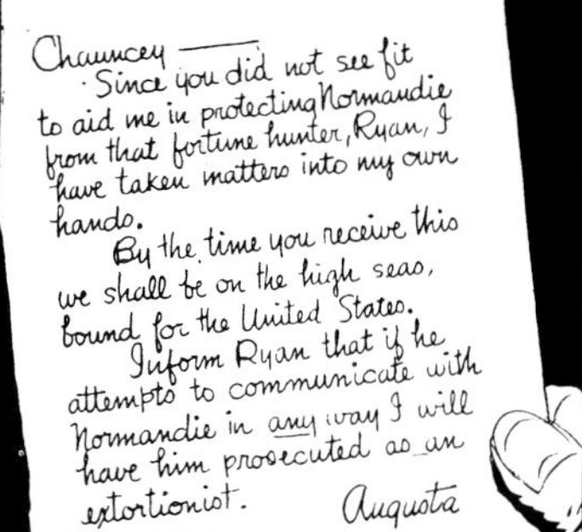
Chauncey —
Since you did not see fit to aid me in protecting Normandie from that fortune hunter, Ryan, I have taken matters into my own hands.
By the time you receive this we shall be on the high seas, bound for the United States.
Inform Ryan that if he attempts to communicate with Normandie in any way I will have him prosecuted as an extortionist.
Augusta

By 1957, Caniff's storytelling had matured, as this short sequence from *Steve Canyon* shows. He demonstrates here a well-controlled flow of story that sustains its connection between strips. His plots are played out with panels that are mostly standard so that they do not intrude graphically. This enhances the flow of the narrative and forces concentration on the actors. In this story, his action-filled episodes accelerate the rhythm of the strip yet allow the dialogue to retain its meter. He uses wordless panels masterfully and composes them so that they invite the reader to participate in the "acting."

PLEASE REGISTER MR. HOGAN INTO MY ROOM—HE HAD ONE TOO MANY TRANQUILIZER PILLS!
Copyright 1957, Field Enterprises, Inc.
9-15

9/16
WH-WHAT'S THIS, COL. CANYON?
JUST WHAT I SAID = PUT MY ROOM ON DOUBLE INSTEAD OF SINGLE RATE! —MR. HOGAN WILL SIGN THE REGISTER WHEN HE RETURNS FROM OUTER SPACE!

SIR, THIS MAN'S BEEN GIVEN KNOCK-OUT DROPS OF SOME KIND! SHOULD I CALL THE HOUSE DOCTOR?
NO...HOGAN HAS SURVIVED WORSE THAN THAT...AND IT PROBABLY TOOK A DOUBLE MICKEY TO CLOBBER HIM!

WHAT WAS HIS TROUBLE—A WOMAN, MONEY, AMBITION—OR JUST PLAIN CUSSEDNESS?
ALL OF THEM—IN ONE DAY! EVEN THE MEN WHO STOOD UNDER THE AIR-TO-AIR ATOMIC ROCKET BURST COULDN'T HAVE HELD UP UNDER SO MUCH PRESSURE!
MILTON CANIFF

9/17
WONDER WHAT HOGAN IS DREAMING ABOUT—THE STUBBORN MUGG...
...HE'S THE SORT OF TOUGH JOKER WHO WINS HERO MEDALS—THEN CAN'T ADJUST TO PEACE! ...HE ALWAYS HAS TO BE FIGHTING WITH SOMEONE!

HE PROBABLY REALLY BELIEVED HE COULD INVADE WESTERN CHINA AND PUT PRINCESS SNOWFLOWER BACK ON HER THRONE!...
I'M SURE HE DIDN'T EVEN THINK ONCE THAT HE COULD TRIGGER WORLD WAR III AND START THE KILLING OF A FEW MILLION PEOPLE!
MILTON CANIFF

WELL—GOTTA GET TO SLEEP... THE ADVENTURES OF PRINCESS SNOWFLOWER ARE CATCHING UP WITH ME!
...AS STEVE GOES TO BRUSH HIS TEETH, HOGAN STIRS—AND OPENS HIS EYES...

9/18
...MAYBE WE CAN GET DOAGIE HOGAN SOME SORT OF JOB...
THAT MUCH ENERGY SHOULD BE WORTH A SALARY TO SOME FIRM...
MILTON CANIFF

WOW! WHAT HAS HAPPENED TO ALL THE MONEY HOGAN HAS COLLECTED FOR SNOWFLOWER'S RE-INVASION OF WESTERN CHINA?...

YOU WOULD THINK OF THAT, CANYON!

There is a major structural difference between newspaper storytelling strips and comic books. In comic books, stories come to a definite conclusion, a tradition that began when the early comic books advertised that each story was complete. A book is free-standing, whereas newspapers are connected to the pattern of daily life. In a daily continuity, therefore, the storyteller need only segue into the next adventure. Caniff understood that the story had to emulate the seamless flow of life's experiences and that the human adventure doesn't have neat endings. His work shows us how to tell a story that could make itself part of the reader's daily life.

THE SHORT/SHORT PLOT

If stories can be extended, they can also be compressed. The success of such a "shortening" lies in the preservation of the essence. The major theme or plot must be preserved, and the collateral dramatization is cut to the bone. In this, the reader supplies the intervening action either by reflexive deduction or drawing from experience.

Ernest Hemingway narrated the shortest short story as follows..."For sale, baby shoes, never used." It would not be hard to write a larger story around this core. The power of this story lies in the skill with which the selection of the "touchstone" points are made. They coopt the reader and immerse him or her in a sea of memory and experience. Cleverly, it forces the reader to "write" the story. The visual here is designed to evoke a setting.

THE ONE-PAGE STORY

As early as 1916, George Herriman, the medium's most innovative storyteller, laid the tracks for the highly-condensed graphic narrative. With *Krazy Kat,* a Sunday comics page, he demonstrated compact story delivery by deploying his images in a format that would influence generations of comic tellers who came after him. The following is an example of this:

Reprinted with special permission of King Features Syndicate

SEPTEMBER 17, 1916

THE ILLUSTRATOR — STORY TELLER

Riding the crest of the wave of adventure story comics, by 1937 the interest in well-drawn (good art) strips opened up Sunday pages to established illustrators. Harold Foster, who for six years had produced a daily strip based on the popular *Tarzan* novels switched to a story of his own. *Prince Valiant* is the story of a young knight in the days of King Arthur. It is peopled with characters drawn from legend and the books of Sir Walter Scott. *Prince Valiant* appeared only a year after the birth of the comic book, where complete stories were being told in the ever-refining sequential art form. In comic books, the trend was to have the story told with images and dialogue balloons with little narrative prose. Foster, however, employed the practice of traditional book illustration. In the literary world, however, classsic book illustration was more highly regarded than comics. It did, after all, leave the text unmolested. The newspapers accommodated this reverence, hiring well-established artists to illustrate stories. The format was comic-related, but the storytelling depended mostly on text. Harold Foster, an accomplished artist, illustrated his stories with splendid, well-researched art that left a minimum text to carry the thread.

Shortly after the feature began, he departed from the partnership of text and image principle so unique to comics. To maintain a story flow under these conditions is very difficult. An early episode demonstrates (see the numbered panels) his groping toward a sequential format to accommodate this kind of narrative. *Prince Valiant* is a classic example of narrative illustration that remains steadfastly in service to the story. It is reader friendly.

In studying the storytelling process of this form of sequential art, one should first note the composition of each panel. Foster maintained the narrative dominance of the art by illustrating the whole of the action. He deployed the actors in a manner similar to the required stagecraft in a sequenced comic. Throughout his stories, the main characters remained in the center of action and Foster avoided highly descriptive prose. Its brevity allowed him to employ art that told a great deal of story. The effectiveness of *Prince Valiant* as narrative illustration is demonstrated by its visual flow. The high degree of accuracy and detail should not be regarded as purely decorative; it is a major ingredient in storytelling.

NEXT WEEK: "THE DRAGON"

42. Harold Foster, "Prince Valiant," 1937. © King Features Syndicate.

Prince Valiant IN THE DAYS OF KING ARTHUR
BY HAROLD R FOSTER
Our Story: EACH MORNING ALETA, QUEEN OF THE MISTY ISLES, MARCHES HER FAMILY DOWN TO THE SEASHORE FOR THEIR SWIMMING LESSON. AND THEY LEARN QUICKLY, FOR THEIR MOTHER IS EQUALLY QUICK WITH THE PALM OF HER HAND OR AN ENCOURAGING SMILE. IT IS ALSO RECORDED THAT MANY YOUNG GALLANTS BECAME INTERESTED IN SWIMMING INSTRUCTION AND CAME TO OBSERVE THEIR LOVELY QUEEN (IN A WET BATHING SUIT) GIVE LESSONS TO HER BROOD.

IT HAS BEEN CLAIMED, AND WITH SOME LOGIC TOO, THAT ALETA'S MOTHER HAD BEEN A MERMAID, FOR BOTH WERE AS MUCH AT HOME IN THE WATER AS IN THE PALACE. NOW, THE LESSON OVER, ALETA GLIDES FAR OUT TO SEA.

PRINCE VALIANT COMES SAILING HOME FROM THE PILGRIMAGE TO THE HOLY LAND. AS THE SHIP NEARS THE MISTY ISLES HE SEES A SPOT OF GOLD GLEAMING AMONG THE SPARKLING WAVES.

WITH A SHOUT OF JOY HE FLINGS ASIDE HIS CLOTHES, HIS CARES AND HIS COMMON SENSE AND LEAPS INTO THE SEA.
COPR. 1954, KING FEATURES SYNDICATE, Inc., WORLD RIGHTS RESERVED.
923 10-17-54

IT IS A WET AND SALTY KISS, BUT QUITE SATISFACTORY.

HAL FOSTER
NOW THAT HE CAN TAKE HER IN HIS ARMS, WHAT DOES THE POOR FOOL DO? HE KNEELS BEFORE HER, TONGUE-TIED, DUMB, HIS HEART POUNDING. BUT THEN HE NEED NOT SPEAK. HIS EYES ARE SAYING QUITE PLAINLY: "I LOVE YOU!"
NEXT WEEK:- Cupid Strikes Again.

THE TOTALLY GRAPHIC STORY

The graphic novel, as we know it today, consists of a combination of text, either narrative or dialogue (balloons) integrated with sequentially deployed art. But early efforts in graphic narrative literature approached this form with an almost total elimination of words.

In Belgium, Frans Masereel, a skilled wood engraver, pioneered in the expansion of this art and employed it as a narrative tool.

In 1927, Masareel's *Die Sonne* was published in Germany. It consisted of 63 plates.

Masareel was joined by German artist Otto Nückel whose wood engravings formed the basis of *Destiny*, a more ambitious (approximately 200 plates) work. This appeared in the United States about 1930.

The story here was more sophisticated and the graphic narrative more complex.

A study of the graphic novel form will reveal that a major burden of narration is assigned to the artwork. But with the proliferation of the comic book, the responsibility for the telling of the story is shared by text and image. The success of this mix of medium quickly succeeded and the totally graphic technique quickly gave way to the familiar graphic novel. A forerunner of the modern graphic novel is found in the work of Lynd Ward. He stands out as perhaps the most provocative graphic storyteller in this century.

Ward was a successful book illustrator famous for his brilliant woodcuts.. In 1937 he published *Vertigo,* a graphic novel narrated entirely with wood engraved images. Without a word of text he succeeds in telling a complete, compelling story thus proving the viability of the form. What is even more significant is that in over 300 pages, *Vertigo*'s only concession to text is the occasional use of signs and posters. Ward kept the narrative focused by titling each chapter with a date. He used the entire page as a panel. Printed on only one side of the leaf, with each image floating in open space, he obliged the reader to turn a page in order to get to the next panel. This gave the reader time to dwell on each image and gave the storyteller total reader engagement.

Vertigo was printed as a conventional book and sold in book stores. It is interesting to note that this occurred about the time the first comic books appeared on newsstands. *Vertigo* was published by a mainstream publisher.

The story requires the reader to contribute dialogue and the intervening flow of action between pages. While this permutation succeeded in demonstrating the viability of graphic storytelling, to an audience alien to comics it could not go very far beyond simply breaking new ground. Many readers found this book difficult to read. Some enjoyed the magnificent effects of his wood cuts. But in the main, this experiment overlooked the reinforcement of a balanced mix of image and text. Ward was obviously not interested in accommodating the great dependence graphic storytelling has on a "prepared" reader already conditioned to participating in the narrating process. The amount of action that transpires between these scenes takes considerable input from the reader to comprehend it. There is a certain "visual literacy" that is second
For the practitioner (writer or artist), *Vertigo* can serve as a skeleton upon which to experiment with a story that has tighter graphic sequencing.

THE GIRL

1929

11

ELECTRONIC DELIVERY

Graphic storytelling via electronic transmission must deal with format and reading rhythm, which is totally different from print.

This is a comic book page. The layout is a traditional arrangement of images, text and panels. The reader arranges the sequence of events in his own mind. A video or CD Rom will take over this task, as it converts this graphic story from print to video.

In order to accommodate to the video rhythm, the art was separated into static scenes supported by sound, music and animated text. Each frame appeared on the screen at intervals lasting as long as it took actors to speak the balloons and the narrator to read the text. But now, the graphic storyteller had to deal with a rhythm of acquisition that is different from print. The rate of speed with which the images appear was out of the viewer's control because they were delivered mechanically. The viewer, therefore, was obliged to retain a memory of each preceding frame. Accompanied by sound and music, each frame appeared in a cadence designed to achieve a sense of motion, suspense and drama. This permitted a certain amount of unconnected art jumping from frame to frame, but it eschewed the use of image connectors normally employed in printed sequential art. The staging or composition of each frame is treated as an independent unit designed to allow the sound to help bridge the action. Absent in this medium is the variety of panel shapes used in print to supply support to the storytelling. Further, the entire display of the 200 frames involved in this story must be delivered within a viewing time of 28 minutes. This, of course, reduces the intellectual participation visually engaged by sequential graphics in print. It becomes a comic book on video — an example of the effect electronic delivery has on graphic storytelling.

AMONG THE CREATURES THAT ROAMED THE ATLANTIC AND PACIFIC OCEANS WAS A HUGE WHITE WHALE..
HE HUNTED THE HUNTERS WITH CUNNING AND INTELLIGENCE
AND STORIES ABOUT HIM BECAME LEGENDARY
WHALING MEN FEARED HIM.. THEY CALLED HIM MOBY DICK....
ONE SPRING I ARRIVED AT THE WHALING PORT OF NANTUCKET IN SEARCH OF A SEAFARING LIFE
THERE I HOPED TO FIND A BERTH ON A SHIP AND HIGH ADVENTURE AT SEA
I MUST FIND LODGING FOR THE NIGHT!!
Spouter INN Peter Coffin
AH HERE IS A LIKELY INN I'LL TRY THIS
AYE, SON WHAT'LL YE HAVE?
A ROOM, SIR.

YOU'LL HAVE TO SHARE A BED WITH A HARPOONER,
AYE IT WILL DO
Spouter INN Peter Coffin
...AND WHAT BE YER NAME SON?
CALL ME ISHMAEL!
LATE THAT NIGHT I AWOKE
MY.. ROOMATE APPEARED
THE HARPOONER.. ULP..
WHAT IS THY NAME
QUEEQUEG!
I KILL MANY WHALE... HA!
?
I BE KING IN MY ISLANDS FAR AWAY
ALL THAT NIGHT I LISTENED AS HE TOLD ME OF HIS LIFE.. WE BECAME FRIENDS

WHAT IS THIS THING -
HERE IS YOJO.. A MIGHTY GOD.. HE SAY YOU FIND A SHIP? FOR US
AYE... MY FRIEND.. AYE
SO.. WE BE FRIENDS AND WE GO TO SEA TOGETHER!
HM.. ZZ- TOMORROW
THE NEXT DAY WE SET OUT ALONG THE WHARVES TO FIND A SHIP
YONDER. IS THE WHALER PEQUOD WE'LL TRY, HER
WELCOME ABOARD! I'M CAPTAIN PELEG AT YER SERVICE!
WE SEEK A BERTH SIR!
D'YE HEAR THAT MR. BILDAD!
AYE BE THEY ABLE?
QUEEQUEG SHOW... SEE THAT SPOT OF OIL IN THE WATER?
AYE

MAHAP IT BE A WHALE...
LOR..
THE SAVAGE IS SKILLED SIGN THEM ON PELEG!
SO WE HAD OUR SHIP
SOON WE'LL SAIL, EH, QUEEQUEG?
AHEM!
I HARPOON HIM LIKE THIS!
?
SIGNED ON THE PEQUOD?? AND HAVE YE MET ITS CAPTAIN.. AHAB YET?
NAY, HE KEPT TO HIS CABIN SICK, I THINK!
HA, WHEN THIS IVORY STUMP OF ME HAND HEALS ...SO WILL HE."
I CAN TELL YE ABOUT HIM... HOW HE LOST HIS LEG.. BUT, WHAT WILL BE WILL BE .. MATES!

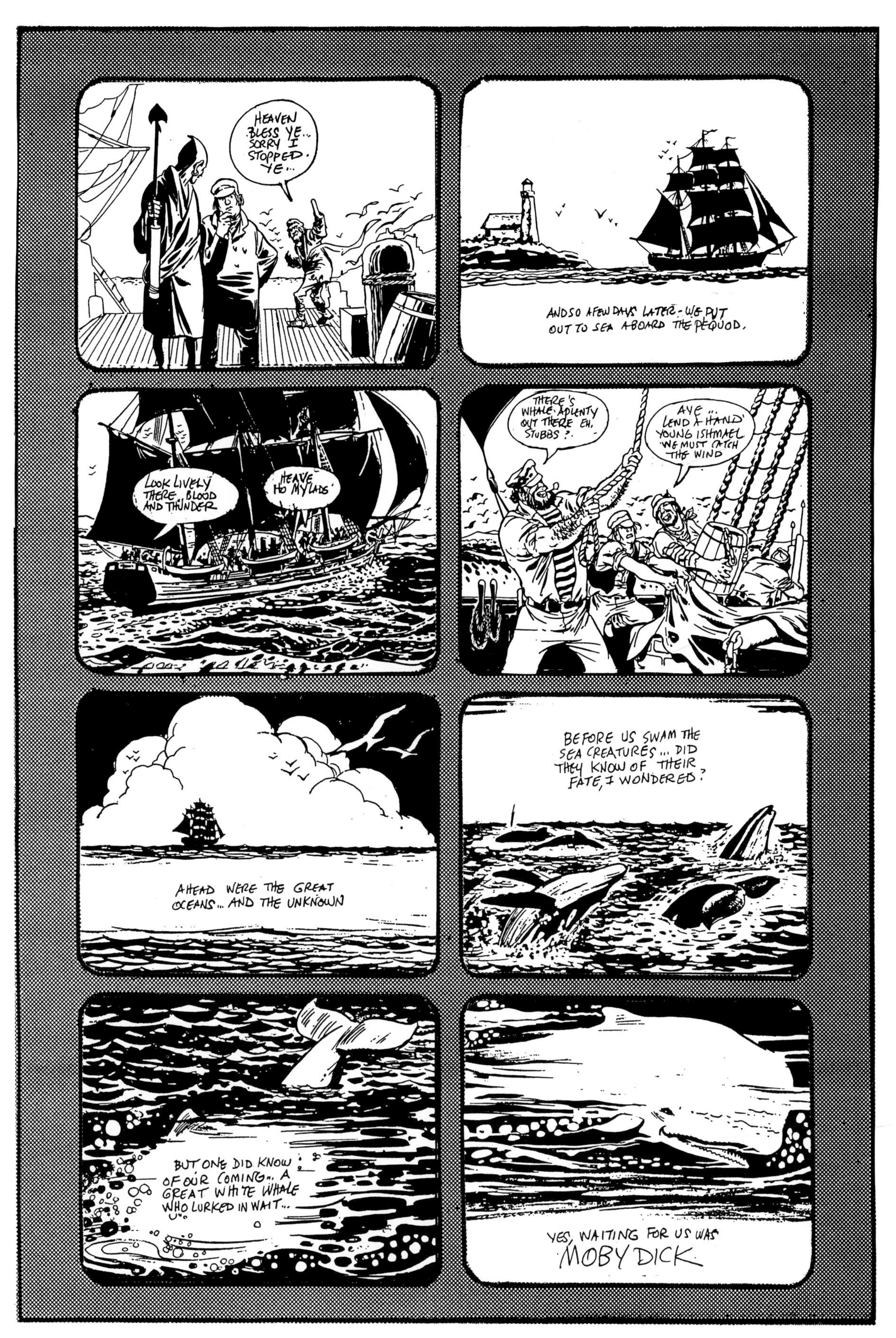
HEAVEN BLESS YE... SORRY I STOPPED YE...
AND SO A FEW DAYS LATER - WE PUT OUT TO SEA ABOARD THE PEQUOD.
LOOK LIVELY THERE, BLOOD AND THUNDER
HEAVE HO MY LADS
THERE'S WHALE APLENTY OUT THERE EH, STUBBS ?.
AYE ... LEND A HAND YOUNG ISHMAEL WE MUST CATCH THE WIND
AHEAD WERE THE GREAT OCEANS... AND THE UNKNOWN
BEFORE US SWAM THE SEA CREATURES... DID THEY KNOW OF THEIR FATE, I WONDERED?
BUT ONE DID KNOW OF OUR COMING... A GREAT WHITE WHALE WHO LURKED IN WAIT...
YES, WAITING FOR US WAS
MOBY DICK

ABOARD THE SPEEDING PEQUOD A MOOD OF MYSTERY SET IN
I BEGAN TO NOTICE STRANGE THINGS..
WHO IS THAT?
HIS NAME IS FEDELLA... HE'S THE CAPTAINS SOOTH SAYER
WHAT SAY YOU OF OUR VOYAGE.. OH, SOOTH SAYER?
I PROPHESY THE CAPAIN WILL DIE ON THIS VOYAGE WITH NEITHER HEARSE NOR COFFIN
MR. STARBUCK WHAT MANNER OF MAN IS OUR CAPTAIN AHAB, WE NEVER SEE HIM
AH... HE'S A STRANGE MAN.. WITH SOMETHING DARK INSIDE HIM!
HE KEEPS TO HIS CABIN!
AH.. YOU WILL SEE HIM SOON ENOUGH BOY!!

12

ART STYLE AND STORYTELLING

Sooner or later, the subject (or question) of art style surfaces in relationship to the process of graphic storytelling. The ratio of its importance to other elements is arguable, but it is an inescapable ingredient. The reality is that art style tells story. Remember, this is a graphic medium and the reader absorbs mood and other abstracts through the artwork. Style of art not only connects the reader with the artist but it sets ambiance and has language value. Do not confuse technique with style. Many artists use crosshatch stippling, dry brush and wash the way a jazz musician might use "riffs." Style, as we define it here, is the artwork's "look" and "feel" in service of its message.

Certain graphic stories are best told with a style appropriate to the content, and they often succeed or fail on that account. This is usually more of a problem for the artist than the writer, since it requires an artist to adopt a style appropriate to the story. There are some artists who can emulate almost any style, but this requires the discipline of a forger. Many contemporary artists engaged in graphic storytelling have an inherent art style compatible to content. Some are capable of mastering different styles to accommodate a story.

Moebius (Jean Giraud), for example, demonstrates a deliberate change of style for two totally different story missions:

BLUEBERRY (Western)

ARZAK (Science Fiction)

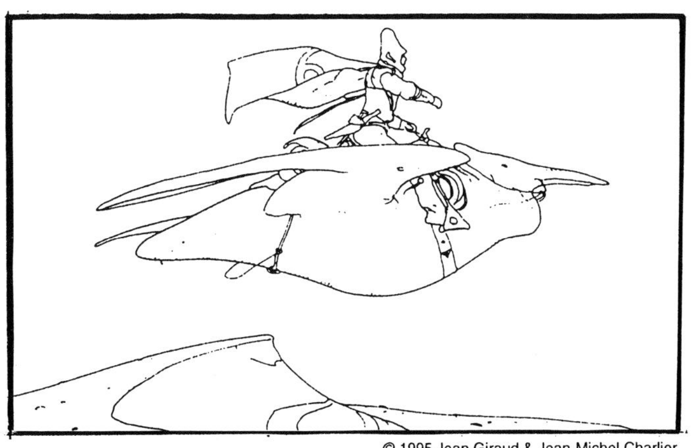

In *MAUS,* Art Spiegelman worked in a style that, because of its character, delivered story. The overall "look" appropriately conveyed the impression that the artwork was created and smuggled out of a concentration camp. This is *graphic storytelling.*

© Art Spiegelman 1984, 1986 from *MAUS, A Survivors Tale,* Pantheon Books

In his illustrations for *Introduction to Kafka,* a biography, Robert Crumb's natural style succeeds as a narrative.

© Published by Totem Books USA

THE VOICE OF THE TELLER

There is a psychic transmission present in the best graphic storytelling. It is generated by the teller's passion. It carries the story's emotional charge to the reader A classic example of that is Al Capp's *Li'l Abner.* One can "feel" the intensity and "hear" the laughter of the teller behind the art. In this segment of daily strips Capp keeps the high voltage story going. The reader laughs even before ingesting the story...which is quite thin.

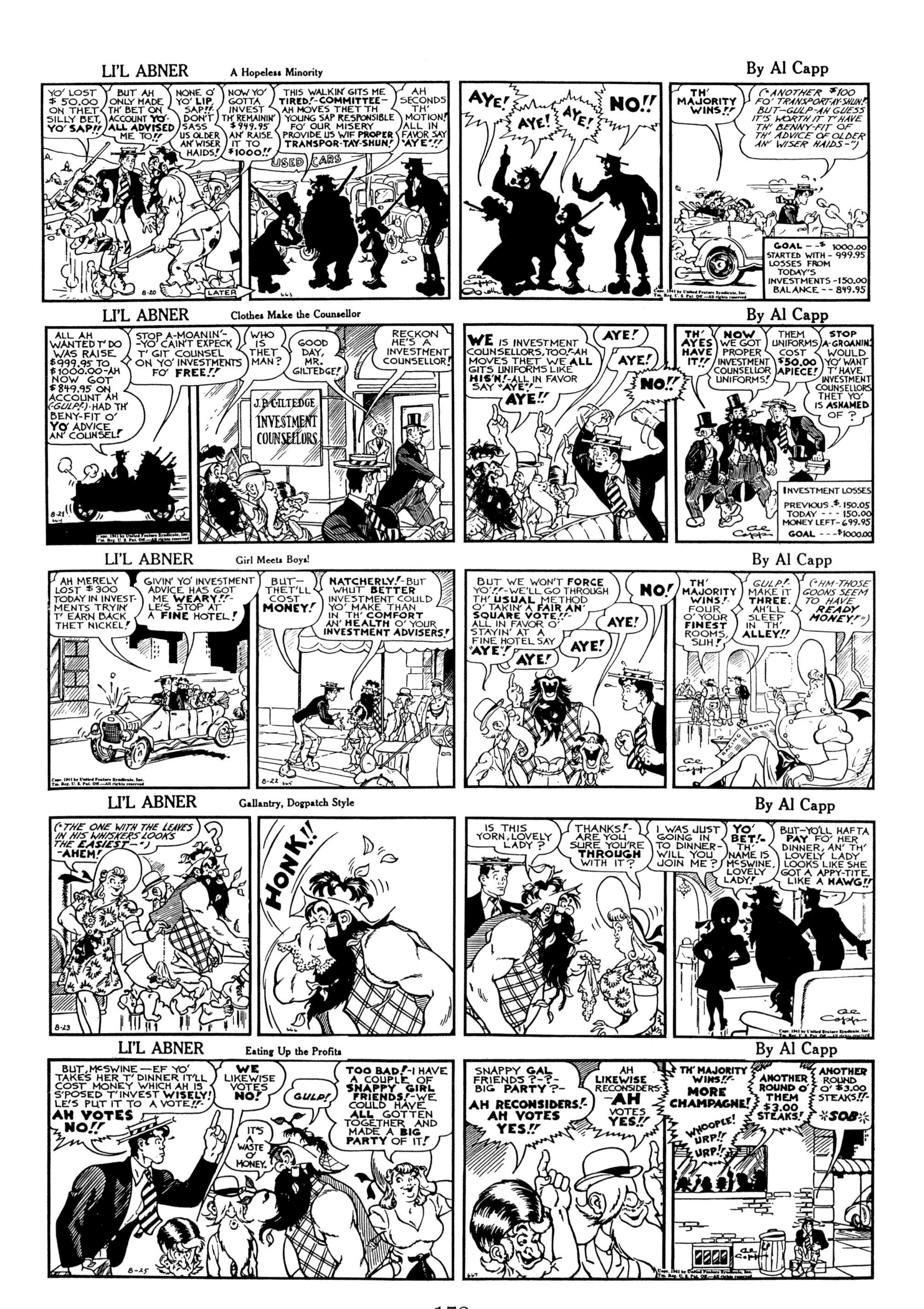

LI'L ABNER
A Hopeless Minority
By Al Capp
YO' LOST $50.00 ON THET SILLY BET, YO' SAP!!
BUT AH ONLY MADE TH' BET ON ACCOUNT YO' ALL ADVISED ME TO!!
NONE O' YO' LIP, SAP!! DON'T SASS US OLDER AN' WISER HAIDS!
NOW YO' GOTTA INVEST TH' REMAININ' $949.95 AN' RAISE IT TO $1000!!
LATER
THIS WALKIN' GITS ME TIRED!-COMMITTEE-AH MOVES THET TH YOUNG SAP RESPONSIBLE FO' OUR MISERY PROVIDE US WIF PROPER TRANSPOR-TAY-SHUN!
AH SECONDS TH' MOTION! ALL IN FAVOR SAY "AYE"!!
USED CARS
AYE!
AYE!
AYE!
NO!!
TH' MAJORITY WINS!!
(*ANOTHER $100 FO' TRANSPORT-AY-SHUN! BUT-GULP-AH GUESS IT'S WORTH IT T' HAVE TH' BENNY-FIT OF TH' ADVICE OF OLDER AN' WISER HAIDS-*)
GOAL - - $ 1000.00
STARTED WITH - 999.95
LOSSES FROM TODAY'S INVESTMENTS - 150.00
BALANCE - - 849.95
LI'L ABNER
Clothes Make the Counsellor
By Al Capp
ALL AH WANTED T' DO WAS RAISE $999.95 TO $1000.00-AH NOW GOT $849.95 ON ACCOUNT AH (-GULP!-)-HAD TH' BENY-FIT O' YO' ADVICE AN' COUNSEL!
STOP A-MOANIN'-YO' CAIN'T EXPECK T' GIT COUNSEL ON YO' INVESTMENTS FO' FREE!!
WHO IS THET MAN?
GOOD DAY, MR. GILTEDGE!
RECKON HE'S A INVESTMENT COUNSELLOR!
J.P. GILTEDGE
INVESTMENT COUNSELLORS
WE IS INVESTMENT COUNSELLORS, TOO!-AH MOVES THET WE ALL GITS UNIFORMS LIKE HIS'N!-ALL IN FAVOR SAY "AYE"!-AYE!!
AYE!
AYE!
NO!!
TH' AYES HAVE IT!!
NOW WE GOT PROPER INVESTMENT COUNSELLOR UNIFORMS!
THEM UNIFORMS COST $50.00 APIECE!
STOP A-GROANIN! WOULD YO' WANT T' HAVE INVESTMENT COUNSELLORS THET YO' IS ASHAMED OF?
INVESTMENT LOSSES
PREVIOUS - $ 150.05
TODAY - - - 150.00
MONEY LEFT - 699.95
GOAL - - - $1000.00
LI'L ABNER
Girl Meets Boys!
By Al Capp
AH MERELY LOST $300 TODAY IN INVEST-MENTS TRYIN' T' EARN BACK THET NICKEL!
GIVIN' YO' INVESTMENT ADVICE HAS GOT ME WEARY!!-LE'S STOP AT A FINE HOTEL!
BUT-THET'LL COST MONEY!
NATCHERLY!-BUT WHUT BETTER INVESTMENT COULD YO' MAKE THAN IN TH' COMFORT AN' HEALTH O' YOUR INVESTMENT ADVISERS!
BUT WE WON'T FORCE YO'!!-WE'LL GO THROUGH TH' USUAL METHOD O' TAKIN' A FAIR AN' SQUARE VOTE!!-ALL IN FAVOR O' STAYIN' AT A FINE HOTEL SAY "AYE"!
NO!
AYE!
AYE!
AYE!
TH' MAJORITY WINS!-FOUR O' YOUR FINEST ROOMS, SUH!
GULP!-MAKE IT THREE. AH'LL SLEEP IN TH' ALLEY!!
(*HM-THOSE GOONS SEEM TO HAVE READY MONEY!*)
RACING FORM
LI'L ABNER
Gallantry, Dogpatch Style
By Al Capp
(*THE ONE WITH THE LEAVES IN HIS WHISKERS LOOKS THE EASIEST-*) -AHEM!
?
HONK!!
IS THIS YORN, LOVELY LADY?
THANKS!-ARE YOU SURE YOU'RE THROUGH WITH IT?
I WAS JUST GOING IN TO DINNER-WILL YOU JOIN ME?
YO' BET!-TH' NAME IS McSWINE, LOVELY LADY!
BUT-YO'LL HAFTA PAY FO' HER DINNER, AN' TH' LOVELY LADY LOOKS LIKE SHE GOT A APPY-TITE LIKE A HAWG!!
LI'L ABNER
Eating Up the Profits
By Al Capp
BUT, McSWINE-EF YO' TAKES HER T' DINNER IT'LL COST MONEY WHICH AH IS S'POSED T' INVEST WISELY! LE'S PUT IT TO A VOTE!!-AH VOTES NO!!
WE LIKEWISE VOTES NO!
GULP!
IT'S A WASTE O' MONEY.
TOO BAD!-I HAVE A COUPLE OF SNAPPY GIRL FRIENDS!-WE COULD HAVE ALL GOTTEN TOGETHER AND MADE A BIG PARTY OF IT!
SNAPPY GAL FRIENDS?-?-BIG PARTY?-
AH RECONSIDERS!-AH VOTES YES!!
AH LIKEWISE RECONSIDERS-AH VOTES YES!!
TH' MAJORITY WINS!!-MORE CHAMPAGNE!
ANOTHER ROUND O' THEM $3.00 STEAKS!
ANOTHER ROUND O' $3.00 STEAKS!!-*SOB*
WHOOPEE!
URP!!
URP!!

AND...THE TELLER

Invariably, the teller becomes identified with and somehow part of the narrative. The uncontrollable elements in this otherwise disciplined medium, including style, selection of stereotypes, portrayal of violence, males, females, and the resolution of conflict, unmasks the teller. The responsibility for the selection of stereotypes, portrayal of violence and the resolution of conflict falls on the teller. Bias and values are revealed through the artwork because the "acting" of the participants in a story emanates from the artist's private memory of human behavior. Contriving the postures and gestures of a heart-broken character reacting to a great misfortune, for example, stems from inside the teller. The graphic storyteller has to be willing to expose himself emotionally.

Sentimentalism, Schmaltz, Violence, Pornography generally characterize a story and are ingredients under the teller's control.

- Sentiment is defined as an attitude resulting from feelings associated with emotion, idealism and nostalgia.
- Schmaltz stems from a Yiddish word for *oily* or *fat* and is associated in storytelling with exploitive emotionalism and excessive pathos.
- Violence portrays the act of physical struggle.
- Pornography, in graphic storytelling, can be defined as excessive exploitation of sexual activity to titillate.

Ultimately, story tellers have a responsibility not only to the reader but to themselves. Stories have influence. This imposes on the teller certain choices. What effect will the story have? Does the teller want to be identified with it? What are the limits of moral standards to which he will adhere.

THE MARKETPLACE

The graphic storyteller cannot escape the marketplace. A comic is essentially visual, which makes its package the product. The artwork influences the initial sale. This is not lost on the retailer and distributor, who are the final access to the reader. This encourages the creators to concentrate on form rather than content. The market, therefore, exercises a creative influence. The graphic storyteller, in pursuit of the market, will give sovereignty to the graphics. The graphic storyteller interested in the retention of readership will keep graphics in service to the story.

AND, FINALLY, THE FUTURE

Ultimately, the graphic storyteller must think about the future of his medium. An ever-advancing technology affects the communication environment.

A capsule history of transmitting graphics demonstrates the validity of this concern. The vehicles used have always been and still are in ceaseless evolution.

I propose, therefore, to conclude this examination of graphic storytelling by posing the following questions:

1. Over time, have the stories people tell been changed by the new methods of transmission?

2. What has been the role of the image in human communication?

3. How has changing technology affected underlying graphic storytelling skills?

4. How many of the classic vehicles of communication have disappeared as a result of advances in delivery?

5. How has electronic and high-tech altered the audience?

These questions do not have simple answers, but thinking about them can help develop a working perspective that is an abiding necessity to a graphic storyteller.

OBSERVATIONS ON STORY

It is not enough for one who undertakes storytelling in a graphic medium to allow the simplicity of technology and artwork to dominate. An underlying understanding of the philosophical terrain into which one ventures is useful when telling stories.

The following thinkers have contributed a body of useful reference to the art of graphic storytelling.

JOSEPH CAMPBELL

Writing in *The Hero With A Thousand Faces*, Joseph Campbell comments on the nature and the story function of myths. He believes that myths are a nuclei out of which stories are fashioned. "Throughout the inhabited world, in all times and under every circumstance the myths of man have furnished; and they have been the living inspiration of whatever else may have appeared out of the activities of the human body and mind. It would not be too much to say that myth is the secret opening through which the inexhaustible energy of the cosmos pour into human cultural manifestation."

Campbell prefaces this by telling us that, "shape-shifting stories, primitive or sophisticated, are marvelously constant. "It is the business of mythology...and of the fairy tale to reveal the specific dangers...of the dark interior way from tragedy to comedy."

For the storyteller employing the hero to tell his stories, he advises, "the mighty hero of extraordinary powers...who is able to lift mountains and fill himself with terrible glory is each of us." Campbell also believes that "...the usual adventure begins with someone from whom something was taken — or who feels that there is something lacking in the normal experiences permitted to the members of his society. This person then takes off on a series of adventures beyond the ordinary to recover what has been lost or to discover some life-giving elixir."

ROGER D. ABRAHAMS

AFRICAN FOLKTALES by Roger D. Abrahams reminds us that Africa has had a long history of storytelling with imagery. This is related to graphics because sculptures, masks, and postures in dance, are used to accompany words and music to transmit the story. In this way, unaided by the easy availability of printing technology, the village historians, entertainers and philosophers, dealt with tribal education and social conduct.

The author, a specialist in folklore, has some observations that are pertinent to the graphic storyteller. He believes, "The fable and its message are one. Stories operate like proverbs, as a means of depersonalizing, of universalizing, by couching the description of how specific people are acting in terms of how people have always acted." Stories in tribal communities intend to reflect the agricultural environment. They are concerned with domestication of crops and cattle. Weather unreliability and scarcity of natural resources leads to hunger and disease so storytelling often reflects the importance of potency as a factor in the proliferation and survival of families. Social bonds are strained or broken by stealing of food or neglect of children in times of crisis. "Therefore, " he says, "no theme is more important or receives more attention than the building of families or friendship ties to provide that strength which in the face of natural disaster or perilous human responses to it, insures a community's survival."

The actors who people these stories are frequently animals whose characteristics are already familiar to their audience. Dramatizations, in dance or pantomime, employ imagery in which masks or costumes that portray animals serve as storytelling tools. As a result, "...throughout Africa there are stories that *belong* to animals. " Mice, hares, spiders and jackals are regarded as clever creatures and are featured in stories that attack or upset rules and boundaries of communal harmony. Such stories serve as an indirect and impersonal means of engaging in deep discussion.

LADISLAS SEGY

Tribal storytelling often reaches beyond the oral and employs art as an accompaniment. African Art is a very clear demonstration of functional imagery. When art is employed as a language, it submits to a discipline quite different, but related to primitive sculpture.

In *African Sculpture Speaks*, Ladislas Segy points out a relationship between art and story in primitive societies. "The African," he states, "lacking writing — carried his mythology — his literature — in his head, transmitting the legends orally from generation to generation. Sculpture was an additional language through which he expressed his inner life and communicated with the invisible world." Virtually every act in their life had its ritual and every rite had its appropriate image. The art produced was more emotional in content than intellectual but was quite utilitarian, according to Segy. Because of the function of sculpture — particularly in masks used in a mime or dance — it related to known stories. Unlike the use of imagery in print, it was not part of a sequential series but rather contained the story in itself. This sculpture was "...speaking in plastic language." The author attributes the focus of this art form (sculpture) to the lack of writing.

E. H. GOMBRICH

In graphic storytelling, the quality of art is an unavoidable consideration. In *Art And Illusion,* E. H. Gombrich discusses some of the psychological considerations in the evaluation of art work. He points to a common belief that artistic excellence is "...identical with photographic accuracy." Thus, he claims, "...aesthetics...has surrendered its claim to be concerned with the problems of convincing representation, the problem of illusion in art." Referring to great masters of the past, who were both great artists and great illusionists, he further points out that the "...history of representation became increasingly mixed up with the psychology of perception." He observes that the inability to copy nature stems from the inability to see it. He finds that "...a figure drawn by one, ignorant of the structure of knitting of bones and anatomy, is different when compared to one who understands these thoroughly...both see the same life but with different eyes." The true miracle of the language of art, he tells us, is that it can teach us to see the visible world afresh and give us the illusion of looking into the invisible realms of the mind.

FURTHER READING

Understandably, the more recent emergence of the graphic dimension in modern storytelling has produced little in our libraries on this discipline. For the practitioner, however, the understanding of storytelling itself is worthy of study for it underlies and precedes the process of narration.

Roger D. Abrahams. *African Folk Tales* New York, Pantheon Press, 1983
Baker & Greene. *Storytelling Art & Technique*: New York, Bowker, 1987 (Storytelling as it is practiced in the U.S.).
Joseph Campbell. *The Hero With A Thousand Faces* Princeton, N.J., Princeton University Press, 1949
E. H. Gombrich. *Art And Illusion* Princeton, N.J. Princeton University Press, 1960
Norma J. Livo. *Storytelling: Process & Practice*: Littleton, Colo., Libraries Unlimited, 1986 (The art of storytelling.)
Michael Roemer. *Telling Stories*: Lanham, Md., Rowman & Littlefield, 1995 (Narrative technique in storytelling.)
Ladislas Segy. *African Sculpture Speaks* New York, Farrar, Straus & Giroux, 1952
Tappan & Parker, Editors. *Narrative and Storytelling*: San Francisco, Jossey-Bass, 1991 (Moral development aspects to storytelling.)

It is an ancient Mariner,
And he stoppeth one of three,
'By thy long grey beard and glittering eye,
Now wherefore stopp'st thou me?'

The guests are met, the feast is set:
May'st hear the merry din.

He holds him with his glittering eye—
The Wedding-Guest stood still,
And listens like a three years' child
The Mariner hath his will.

The Wedding-Guest sat on a stone:
He cannot choose but hear;
And thus spake on that ancient man,
The bright-eyed Mariner.

"The Ancient Mariner
Samuel Taylor Coleridge